Blood Brother Swan Sister

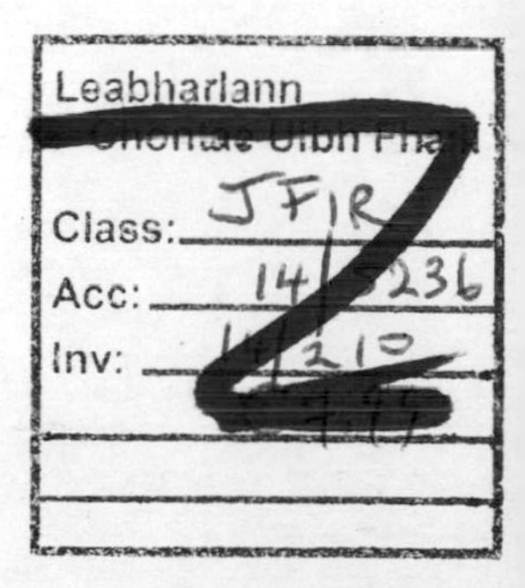

Eithne Massey has written several successful novels for young readers on historical topics: *The Silver Stag*, set in Bunratty Castle, *Where the Stones Sing*, set in Christ Church, Dublin, *The Secret of Kells*, *The Dreaming Tree*, as well as a collection of stories, *Best-loved Irish Legends*.

FOR JACQUES

Blood Brother Swan Sister

EITHNE MASSEY

THE O'BRIEN PRESS
DUBLIN

First published 2014 by The O'Brien Press Ltd.
12 Terenure Road East, Rathgar,
Dublin 6, Ireland.
Tel: +353 1 4923333; Fax: +353 1 4922777
E-mail: books@obrien.ie.
Website: www.obrien.ie
ISBN: 978-1-84717-567-0

1 2 3 4 5 6 7 8 9 10
14 15 16 17 18 19 20

Cover image courtesy of istockphoto
Printed and bound by CPI Group (UK) Ltd, Croydon, CR0 4YY
The paper in this book is produced using pulp from managed forests

The O'Brien Press receives assistance from

CONTENTS

Prologue page 7

PART 1: 16–17 April 1014

1 The End of the March 15

2 The Irish Camp 21

3 The Creature in the Moonlight 26

4 Voyage's End 35

5 Meeting in the Marketplace 43

PART 2: 18–19 April 1014

6 The Meeting in the Woods 53

7 In the City of Dublin 63

8 Around the Fire 69

PART 3: 21–22 April 1014

9 The Locked Chest 83

10 Tomar's Grove 94

11 Magic or Madness? 102

12 The Queen's Task 108

13 The King's Blessing 117

14 The Rider on the Shore 125

15 In the House of the Wise Woman 131

PART 4: 23 April 1014

16 Call to Arms 147

17 The Meadow of the Bull 152

18 The Witch in the Wood 165

19 At the Weir of the Tolka 175

20 The Ring of Tomar 179

21 Easter Saturday-Sunday 1014 192

Historical Note 199

PROLOGUE

Dara woke abruptly. The moon was above the trees, high and full. All around him lay the sleeping soldiers. The camp was silent except for the occasional grunt from one of the sleepers or the soft whimper of a dreaming dog.

Dara felt instantly and totally awake. He knew this feeling from many nights spent outside in the wild places. There was something or someone near him. Watching him.

He sat up and looked across into the shadows of the great oak trees that surrounded the ruined monastery. As silently as he could, he got up and peered into the darkness, pulling out his knife. Bent towards the ground to keep out of the moonlight, he began creeping quietly towards the oak trees. He thought he could see something moving below the trees, creating a rustle in the young ferns and pale spring grass.

He blinked: something white moved in the moonlight. Some kind of animal? Was it a cat? But it was too big, too long, to be any cat he had ever seen. Could it be a stoat? But Dara knew that there were no white stoats in Ireland; the king's white furs had come from the far north, the homelands of the Norsemen. Maybe this one had escaped from a Norse ship?

The creature was behaving in a most peculiar manner, leaning over the faces of the sleeping soldiers. For all the world, it looked as if it was whispering something in their ears.

Elva ran along the banks of the Liffey, cursing silently when the prickly gorse and hawthorn caught in her cloak. She had woken that night to see shards of moonlight shining through the tiny gaps in the wattle wall of the house. Once again her sister was missing from her place beside her in their bed.

It had happened before and Elva had lain awake for hours, waiting for Arna to come back. She had finally fallen asleep and in the morning had found that Arna was back, curled up asleep beside her. Elva poked her awake.

'Where did you go off to, last night?' she asked as soon as Arna opened sleepy eyes, eyes which immediately narrowed in anger.

'What? I was here asleep all night. You must have been having one of your stupid dreams,' she said, her voice sarcastic. Everyone knew that Elva had strange dreams.

'It wasn't a dream,' Elva insisted. 'I woke up and you were gone.'

Arna took Elva's shoulders in her hands and pinched them hard, staring into her sister's eyes with her own fierce silvery ones.

'I wasn't gone anywhere, do you understand?' she said. 'And don't you dare tell your crazy dreams to my father or your mother!'

This time, when Elva woke up, she was determined to find out what was going on. She felt the hollow beside her in the bed. Yes, it was still warm, which meant that Arna was not long gone. She pulled on her calfskin boots and saffron cloak, and whispered fiercely at Pingin, her terrier, who was raising his ears in puzzlement, to stay exactly where he was and keep guard. She crept out past the sleeping dogs and servants and was just in time to see her sister take the route down towards the tunnel in the walls, where the river flowed out of the city.

She had to be very careful creeping through the tunnel behind her, but Elva could be as silent as a cat when she wanted and managed to keep Arna in sight without being seen herself. She was helped by the fact that Arna seemed half-asleep as she moved, as if she were walking in some kind of trance. Elva followed her sister through the meadows that ringed the city, past horses and cows that were not disturbed by the sight of two girls moving quietly in the moonlight.

But when Arna started to make her way through the woods towards the Irish camp, Elva almost turned back. Every child in Dublin had been terrorised by stories of the savage Irish gathering outside the walls, creatures more frightening than wild boars or even wolves. If she and her sister were caught by these soldiers, they would surely be murdered, or at the very least sold as slaves.

But when Arna reached the camp it was as if some kind of spell had been laid on the soldiers. Nobody woke; no guard dog sounded the alarm. The bodies of the men and youths lay on the ground, wrapped in their cloaks, some of them snoring gently. And there was her sister, leaning over them, one by one, as if whispering or breathing something into their ears ...

And then the boy sat up. He had his back to Elva so he didn't see her, but his waking had made her sister disappear into the shadows. She followed them both, impressed by the boy's skill at woodcraft, which was as good if not better than her own. He moved silently through the trees, making no sound at all. At one stage he stopped and turned as if he'd heard something behind him and she stood still, scarcely daring to breathe. When they reached the Liffey, Elva saw Arna slip into the water and disappear in a shaft of moonlight.

Then the boy turned and saw her, where she stood shivering in the cold April air.

PART ONE
16–17 APRIL 1014

LAUGERDAGR, SUNNUDAGR
DÉ SATHAIRN, DÉ DOMHNAIGH
SATURDAY, SUNDAY

CHAPTER 1

THE END OF THE MARCH

Dara stopped at the top of the ridge and caught his breath. Was it possible to actually burst with excitement? If so, he must be very close to it. In the distance, he could see smoke rising, mingling with the mist above the roofs of Dublin. It was so cold that when he breathed out, his breath created its own little patch of mist in the blue air. Far below him, water glinted through green branches. The course of the river showed their way forward, leading to the town and the sea beyond. Most important of all, it showed the way to King Brian's camp. The end of the journey.

Dara could just make out the shape of the walls that circled Dublin. It was certainly bigger than the only other town he had seen, Limerick. But Dara felt a twinge of disappointment – from here the town didn't look *that* impressive. A huddle of low houses, the walls of the Norse king's palace rising above them. One or two spires, Christian churches. He jumped as he felt a hand on his shoulder, shaking him out of his dream. Turlough's voice was full of excitement.

'There it is, Sitric Silkbeard's kingdom,' he said. 'That's where the Norsemen and the Leinstermen are gathered. Just waiting for us to attack. Whoohoo! When we do they won't know what hit them! We'll show them all that my grandfather King Brian really is the high king of all Ireland. We'll be heroes like the warriors of Glen Mama.'

Dara grinned back at his friend. Both he and Turlough had been too young to fight in the great battle of Glen Mama four years ago but they had listened to many tales and songs about the glorious victory. The Munstermen had trounced the Leinstermen and their Dublin allies. Now, finally, they were going to be part of one of those heroic stories. Part of what was perhaps the greatest adventure of all, because if King Brian Boru won this war, no-one would challenge him again. Instead, Sitric and his Norsemen and Mael Mordha and his Leinstermen would pay tribute to Brian as high king. 'I can't wait for the battle to start!' Dara said, grinning from ear to ear.

Dara's father and his uncle Cormac joined them at the ridge. Both men had been on many campaigns with Brian

Boru. Dara's father smiled at his young son and said, 'Well, ye will have to wait a bit yet. Come on, lads, we still have a way to go, so we need to get moving. It's all ahead of us … we will drive the Northmen into the sea and watch them swim for their lives! You have shown your courage on this march, Dara, and I'm proud of you. And I know I will be even prouder of you after this battle. And as for you, Turlough, your father and your grandfather already know your worth, but soon you will be known everywhere as one of the bravest princes of Dal Cais.'

Turlough's father was Murrough, King Brian's chosen heir. Both boys smiled shyly, a little embarrassed by such high praise, but determined to live up to it.

'The sea is beyond Dublin, isn't it?' said Dara, trying to peer through the mist. 'I can't see it yet.'

'No, we won't even be able to see it from our camp tonight,' said his father. 'The main part of the army is camping in the woods and fields to the north, near the coast. We have been told to stay on this side of the river, at Kilmainham, in case any Leinstermen come up from the south or west. But King Brian has promised he will visit us today or at the latest, tomorrow. So, as I said, it's time to move. Shift yourselves!' He called out loudly, 'Men, march on!'

All around him, men and boys picked up their packs and hoisted them onto their backs. Sighing, Dara did the same. The leather straps dug into his shoulders, rubbed raw from weeks of its weight. His feet slipped in the wet soles of his sandals and he wondered if they would ever feel dry again. They had marched along the Great Road from Brian's kingdom in Dalcassia, in the West of Ireland, and it had been a long and a hard march. Dangerous too, once they had reached the territory of the Leinstermen. It was up to everyone to watch out for the enemy, lurking in the forests all around them. It was also up to everyone to carry their own weapons and equipment, for the pack ponies were used only for heavy gear such as cooking pots and spare weapons, and very few were allowed the privilege of riding the horses.

Dara had walked until his feet were blistered, his back ached and his hands had cramp from holding onto his pack. But he knew better than to complain. It was a great honour to march as part of King Brian Boru's army and Brian's soldiers never complained. Well, except Niall. Dara's friend, Niall, complained quite a lot. But he was not on this march. He had been sent east earlier in the spring and Dara had missed him. He couldn't wait to see him again. For some weird reason, it was easier to be cheerful when Niall was around moaning about everything and falling over his feet.

One of the men suddenly burst out singing, and the rest joined in. It lifted Dara's spirits as he marched. Every time they sang together on the march it made him feel so happy to be part of this army, all of them facing danger together.

He raised his head from the muddy track, and saw a flock

of swans flying down the valley. How very much easier it would be if armies could fly!

Still singing, the company marched steadily along the river valley, deeper into the trees that clustered to the west of the city. The cover still let plenty of light through, even though it was late April. Dara imagined that in high summer it must be like travelling through a green, underground tunnel. The wood was full of the sound of birdsong, and thrushes and blackbirds peered at them through the branches or flew across their path as the noise of marching feet and singing voices disturbed them from their nests. They passed hawthorn trees, just starting to bloom, and patches of blue haze where the bluebells were opening out. It had been a long, cruel winter and Dara saw that there were still clumps of primroses in the deepest shade. Then one of them took flight and he realised it was not a flower at all, but a yellow butterfly. The first he had seen this year. Surely a good omen?

He caught up with Turlough. He wanted to ask him about Kilmainham.

'Isn't it where Brian camped before Christmas? When he had to give up the siege of Dublin because the weather got too cold and they ran out of food?'

Turlough nodded. 'That's it. There are the remains of an old monastery there and it's close to the Liffey. The king likes it at Kilmainham: he will probably attend mass there tomorrow, for Palm Sunday. The city walls are only a mile or so to the east. So don't go wandering off on your own, Dara. There may be scouts from the Norse armies around. They say the warriors from the Isle of Man will stick a dagger in you as soon as look at you.'

CHAPTER 2

THE IRISH CAMP

The camp at Kilmainham was buried in the forest on the banks of a small river, which Turlough told Dara was called the Camac. As soon as they arrived, there was a shout of delight and Dara was enveloped in a bear-hug from Niall, who, in his enthusiasm, managed to knock him over. Dara lay on the ground laughing, hardly able to pull himself up because of the weight of his pack. This kind of thing was only to be expected from Niall; the weapons master had once described him as having not just two left feet, but two left arms as well.

Niall pulled his friend up and clapped him on the shoulder. 'You made it! Brilliant!'

Dara grinned back. 'I did! My father finally talked my mother into letting me come with the army … Now, tell me everything! What have I missed?'

'Where do I start? Well, the first thing is that some of us will be moving camp from here to the main camp, further north. The ground is more open there. Better for fighting!' Niall shivered dramatically. 'But part of the land up there is wooded too; I hope we won't be sent to sleep there. That's where Tomar's Wood is. The ghosts of dead Norse soldiers haunt it. It's horrible – always foggy and cold there. It used to be one of the Norse holy places until Malachy of Meath burnt it and cut it to bits a few years ago. But there's still enough left of it to be scary. They say the trees themselves hate the Irish! Anyway, Malachy's armies have come down to join us there. And in Dublin, King Sitric has called in his friends and relations from the other Norse kingdoms and they're gathering in the bay and the river. Dublin is full of their ships,' Niall finally paused to draw breath, but only for a moment. 'Their ships are amazing looking. We should try to get on a scouting party and get down to the bay to have a look. I've told everyone how good you are at scouting, Dara, how quiet you can be when you move through the woods.'

'But they probably won't let us go – we are hardly let go anywhere. It's a pain.'

Niall pulled a face. 'We're not even supposed to go east of the big boundary stone that marks the edge of the monastery. So we're stuck here, my friend. To be honest, it's been boring, just waiting for something to happen. We get all the horrible jobs too, because we're the youngest. And the food is terrible. And I'm really sick of sleeping on the ground …'

Dara grinned. Same old Niall.

His friend continued: 'But now that the armies have come from Meath and your lot from Dalcassia, things are bound to get exciting!'

Dara hoped Niall was right. But despite himself he felt a shiver run down his spine. There was a part of him that was anxious. He had never fought in a battle before. He had nearly been left at home with the children, until finally his father had agreed to let him come along. His mother had not been happy with the decision. His father had said: 'We can't molly-coddle him forever, Lia. He is a Dalcassian, born to fight for his king. I know it's hard to see him go into danger. But there is danger at home too.'

His mother said nothing more. She knew only too well the dangers that lurked everywhere, threatening her children, even close to home. Like the Shannon River, the river they all loved, that had taken Ronan in a flash-flood only the previous winter. And Dara had desperately wanted to get away. Away from his mother's fussing. Away from memories of his older brother Ronan. To a place where he could show his father he was just as brave a son and good a warrior as his brother. And now here he was.

There was a shout from Cormac: 'Come on, lads, less talk and more work! We have to set up camp before dark!'

Dara soon discovered that what Niall had said was true. Because he was one of the youngest soldiers, he was considered everyone's dogsbody. After a boring and back-breaking hour gathering branches, he was sent on errands, bringing messages to different people around the camp. This was better, as it meant that he was able to explore. Thousands of warriors had come from all parts of Ireland, to fight with the high king. As he ran from one chieftain to another, Dara heard bits of gossip about the plans for the attack. He noticed that there were even some Norse soldiers in the camp, fighting on Brian's side. Mostly they were there for gold rather than out of any loyalty towards Brian. But some Norsemen, like Ospak of the Isle of Man, had come to support the high king because they believed that his war was a just one.

Late in the evening Dara finally came upon his father, who was looking worn and tired. Cathal ruffled his son's hair and told him to be sure to wrap up warm against the cold spring nights. They looked at each other and laughed: that was what his mother always said. Cathal smiled ruefully. 'You had better do it! For I told her I would be as careful of you as she would be – and so I will be, as much as I can.'

'There's no need to mind me, Father, I can look after myself,' said Dara reproachfully.

'Let's hope you're right in that, son. But you're so young still … however, you have courage and will enough for a grown man. I just hope that will be enough to get you through the battle and safe home.'

By now, the camp was fully set up and the army feasted by the light of the dozens of fires, pinpricks of brightness scattered throughout the trees. Dara was glad of the warmth and light of the flames. Above them the round moon rose, just visible through the web of branches. Dara grew drowsy, dozing in the heat of the fire, only half-listening as men sang the familiar fighting songs and told old stories of the Fianna. Curled up in his cloak, he felt warm and protected. His cloak was blue, the colour of King Brian's standard. The colour of his one blue eye, his mother had said. She had woven the cloak especially for him. Through half-open eyes he saw that his companions were stretching out on the ground, wrapped up tightly against the night cold. Their cloaks were both their tent and their bedclothes. It had been a long day. His eyes closed and he fell into an exhausted sleep.

CHAPTER 3

THE CREATURE IN THE MOONLIGHT

Dara stood shivering in the cold wind that came up the river. It had been so strange, waking from deep sleep to see the white creature creeping around the sleeping soldiers. But when it crept from the camp Dara had followed it, out of the woods and down to where the grass was smooth and sloped towards the river. As soon as it reached the Liffey, the creature gave a twist of its head, as if looking back at Dara, and then leapt into the water with hardly a splash. Dara could just about see its shape swimming through a path of moonlight towards the opposite side of the river. The moon, reflected on the water, dazzled his eyes and he blinked. When he opened them again there was no sign of the creature. There was only a swan sailing serenely towards the farther bank.

Dara suddenly felt very cold. There had been something uncanny about the white creature. And this place was strange too. All around him the earth was scattered with long green mounds. Dara knew the mounds covered the bodies of dead Norse soldiers. He remembered the stories he had heard, that these sleeping warriors were neither truly alive nor truly dead. That they sometimes took the shape of animals and lured the innocent away to their underground kingdoms. Dara shivered again. Was the white creature one of them?

Now other stories crowded his brain, stories about Norse witches, the shape shifters who could take different forms and lead travellers to their doom. The thought of the creature peering at his companions from the shadows, snuffling at their necks, was horrible.

There was a noise from behind him and he turned, knife at the ready. Someone was watching him from the wood. This was no animal though, but a girl: a girl his own age or perhaps a little younger. Her cloak was the colour of saffron. She was demanding, in Gaelic but with a strange accent, 'Who are you? What are you doing here?'

'And who are you? Are you one of them?' Dara swallowed hard and pointed at one of the Norse barrows.

The girl laughed. 'I should think not! I'm neither dead

nor really Norse, though I do live in Dublin, and my father was from the Norse lands. You must be one of the army of madmen from Dalcassia, come to kill us all. So they tell us.' She didn't sound too worried about the prospect. In fact, she sounded as if she was laughing at him.

He drew himself up as tall as he could. 'I am indeed from Dalcassia, but I am not mad and none of us would kill a child like you. We fight warriors in honourable battles.'

The girl snorted. 'My mother says there is nothing too honourable about men and boys slashing each other to pieces. And if all the warriors are the same age as you I don't think us Dubliners need worry too much. But what are you doing here? What did you see? Did you see something go into the water?'

Dara nodded. 'There was some strange kind of white animal. It led me from the camp. It has disappeared though, into the river. It's very odd – I never saw anything like it before. But what are *you* doing here? Surely you should be in bed, safe behind the walls of Dublin?'

The girl grinned. 'Oh, I have my ways of getting out.' Her face suddenly changed. 'In fact, I'm looking for my sister. She disappeared earlier on and … I'm worried about her. Look, I'd better get back. What's your name, bog boy?'

Despite the insult, the grin on the girl's face made Dara grin back. 'I'm Dara. And who are you? And do you know what the creature in the camp was?'

'I'm Elva, daughter of Weland the Blacksmith and Birgit the Healer. Drop into us when your army takes over Dublin – not that that is going to happen any time soon!' She grinned again. 'As to the white creature you saw – well, I'm hoping I'm wrong, but that … that just might be the sister I'm looking for.'

And then she was gone then, disappearing into the forest like a ghost.

Elva ran back towards Dublin and the safety of its walls. She was so tired. But she knew she had to hurry. She reached the bridge and from there scrambled up the banks to the high walls of the city. She had told no-one about her secret way in and out of Dublin, where one of the offshoots of the Salach River made a channel deep under the walls. She had found it while playing near the Black Pool, and wondered who had dug out the earth over the water. Had it been dug as a way in or a way out? She had thought she was the only person who knew about it, until she had seen Arna using it tonight.

It was not pleasant, crawling through the dark earthy tunnel, and it left her wet and dirty when she pulled herself out on the other side. But she had no time to clean herself up. She had to be back in bed before anyone in the longhouse woke up. If her mother, always the first to rise, saw her coming in, she would be in serious trouble. Birgit's daughters were not allowed out in the night, when every respectable citizen of Dublin was locked in their houses, safe from harm. Especially at the moment, when Dublin was surrounded by soldiers on all sides.

With the coming of the armies, the city had changed. Dubliners were used to visitors from all over the Norse world, but not squads of soldiers, fully armed, filling the streets with their loud voices and strange accents. There was a part of her that found the unrest and bustle quite exciting. But she worried about her father, because he seemed so anxious about the coming war. She had never seen him like this before, and he had looked after her for almost as far back as she could remember. Before they moved into Weland's house, there had been some really bad times. She and her mother had been hungry and cold and some people had spat on her mother because she was Irish, when she begged for food, huddled against the walls of Dublin. With Weland, everything was free from shadows. Or so it had been until last winter, when Dublin was put under siege. Even when King Brian went back to Dalcassia, abandoning the siege, Weland shook his head and told Elva their troubles were not over yet. And he had been right. Now the king's army had come back with the spring, and Dublin held its breath, waiting to see who would win the war, and what its fate would be.

Elva was also worried about her mother, who also seemed especially anxious just now. It was partly the danger from the Irish, but Elva knew she was even more worried about something closer to home. Or rather someone: Arna. Elva's own biggest worry was Arna, who was becoming more and more peculiar.

Arna, with her strange silver eyes and her silent ways. Arna, her half-sister, Weland's daughter. When Elva had first met her, Arna had frowned at her from where she was hiding behind Weland, holding tight to her father's hand. That was when Elva and her mother came to live in Weland's house. Elva had thought that Arna looked sad, and had run to her to hug her, but Arna had pulled away and just held tighter to her father. Arna was older than Elva and much cleverer. So clever that when they quarrelled, it always seemed to be Elva who got into trouble with her mother, even if she had only responded to Arna's needling or a sneaky pinch on the back of her arm. Her mother, in any case, always explained away Arna's bad behaviour by the fact that she had lost her mother so young. Weland never spoke about his first wife, but Elva knew that she had been pure Norse. Arna was very proud of the fact that she had not a drop of Irishness in her. Only a few days ago, she had called Elva a mongrel, because her father had been Norse and her mother was Irish. Elva hadn't understood why her sister was being so mean to her, especially as Arna was the one who had so often defended her little sister from the insults that some of the Dublin children shouted at her because of her mixed race. She had been furious, flinging herself at Arna until her mother came and pulled them apart.

Weland had laughed when he was told the story. 'There's nothing wrong with being a mix of breeds!' he said. 'The dogs that are mixed are often the cleverest and the healthiest, you know!'

'So Elva is a dog, then?' said Arna nastily, looking at her father scornfully. It was one of those looks that could curdle milk. That was what Beorn, the fishmonger's son, had once said of Arna. He had been the victim of one of Arna's special looks because he had asked her to be his girlfriend. Not that Elva could blame her for saying no – Beorn's nose was always dripping and he smelt of fish. But it wasn't just Beorn that Arna looked down on: none of the boys of Dublin were good enough for her. She treated them all with contempt; so much so that they called her names and had once thrown a dead seagull after her in the street.

That was why Elva was so puzzled by her sister's disappearing night after night. With anyone else, she would have suspected that she was meeting a boy. But not Arna. And from what Elva had seen tonight, it seemed that Arna did nothing more than go to look in the faces of the soldiers of the Irish camp. Why? Was she looking for someone? wondered Elva, and if she was, why would that person be in the Irish camp? Arna hated the Irish. And what had she been doing, bending over them? What had she whispered into their ears?

Elva shivered as she ran. She had once seen Arna do something like that to a strange dog that had come up to them drooling and growling, when they had been sitting together on the banks of the Liffey. An odd look had come into Arna's eyes. Then she had lifted up one of the dog's ears and blown into it, whispering words Elva could not hear. And the dog had gone mad, tearing around in circles and howling, as if in pain. He had finally given himself a tremendous shake and jumped into the river. Elva tried to speak to her mother about what had happened – she had been the only one to see what Arna had done. Her mother, as usual, had refused to listen.

But now Elva had reached the longhouse. It was a fine building, and always warm, for Weland was a smith and kept a fire burning in the smithy next door all the time. He was one of the most skilful craftsmen of the city, a whitesmith working in gold and silver, as well as a blacksmith working in iron. As Elva crept into the house, the wolfhound, Rolf, raised his head sleepily from his paws. He made no further movement or sound when Elva held up a warning finger. Pingin whimpered with joy when he saw her and she tucked him into the space her knees made when she curled up in the bed.

She saw that there was someone there already: Arna was fast asleep in the moonlight, looking as if nothing could disturb her peaceful rest.

CHAPTER 4

VOYAGE'S END

'Land! Land at last!' Skari, from his perch in the stern of the boat, called it out as loudly as he could. He heard the cheers behind him as the rowers gave thanks to Thor for a safe arrival. The wind had been against them all the way from Orkney. Old Hravn One-Eye had spent the entire voyage muttering to himself that it was a bad omen.

'It's the Irish demons trying to keep us away from their land, that's what it is,' he declared. 'This journey was cursed from the start.'

Skari's father had told One-Eye to keep his thoughts to himself. The men didn't need to listen to the voice of doom from the corner of the boat where the old man spent his days. They were already so weary from rowing that everyone, jarl and foot-soldier alike, had had to take a turn at the oars.

Skari's own hands were blistered and sore from where the salt water had stung them. By far the youngest soldier on the boat, he had been stuck doing more than his fair share of rowing. But he did not complain; that was not the way of his family, who served Sigurd, Jarl of the Orkneys. Nor was it the Norse way. Those Norse ways had made their people powerful all over the northern seas. Their courage and daring had brought them adventure, and wealth from the farms and monasteries they had raided. It had made them rich with gold and beautiful jewels and even slaves taken from others weaker than they were.

Nowadays there was less raiding and more trade, but the older warriors still spoke of the old days with regret, and were more than happy to tell Skari tales of times past. These stories were part of the reason Skari had been so eager to come on this adventure with his father. And his father had finally given in to his pleas. His best friend – well, if he were honest, his only friend, Hermund – had wanted to come too, but Hermund's mother had made such a fuss that in the end his father had refused him permission. Skari's own stepmother, Ingrid, had not been at all happy to see him go, and his sister, little Gudrun, had cried her eyes out. He had hugged her and said he would be back soon. He had promised that when he did he would take her swimming with him under Lambsfell, where the seals came out of the sea caves and played in the water.

Now he wiped the salty spray from his eyes and peered into the distance. A dim line of blue hills appeared to the south. To the north he could see the jutting nose of Howth. The sky was pale, the colour of milk. Fields, some of them full of cattle, some with sheep and lambs grazing, some of them ploughed for sowing, lined the shore. They were patched with spring gold, buttercups and gorse. Behind them were forests, stretching into the distance as far as the eye could see. Skari, from the windswept Orkneys, had never seen so many trees. But it was the bay itself that was the most interesting part of the view. Already it was filled with ships, fleets from the Isle of Man, from York, from as far away as Friesland and Norway itself. All had come to support the King of Leinster and their kinsman, Sitric of Dublin, in their bid to break the power of Brian Boru forever. And there would be rich rewards for their efforts.

As they rowed further into the bay he could see the huddle that was Dublin itself, built on the south bank of the river and surrounded by walls of earth and wickerwork, patched with stone here and there. It was bigger than any of the settlements in Orkney. Dublin was a famous trading town. It was a crossroads where anything could be bought or sold: furs from the north, amber and dried fish from the east, and, from the south, spices and gold and fine cloths. Yes, anything could be bought and sold in Dublin, including people. Skari's mother had been bought here.

Old One-Eye was muttering to himself again, chanting a poem. Skari shivered. One-Eye was treated with respect by everyone. He had secret wisdom. He could read the runes and the signs of weather, could even foretell the future, which was why he had been brought along on the voyage. He certainly had not been brought for the pleasure of his company.

Skari never felt comfortable around him. He wished he had not been put in the same boat as him, for One-Eye seemed to single him out for special attention. It was probably because Skari was different too; his odd-coloured eyes – one green, one blue – set him apart, and made people think he might have special powers. Skari sometimes thought that if he had such powers, he wished they would hurry up and make themselves known!

The fleet passed a small island, then the Tolka River and a huddle of fisherman's huts on the shoreline. The mouth of the Liffey was wide, with swamp and slob lands stretching on either side. There were more ships moored here, beautiful boats with carved prows. The ship passed dragons with open jaws and serpents with their heads raised to strike, prancing seahorses and sea monsters with red, curling tongues and bulging blue eyes. Shouts of greeting came across the water as they landed the boats upriver by the walls of the town.

There at the gates stood King Sitric himself and his

nobles, come to greet Jarl Sigurd. Skari stared hard at Sitric Silkbeard. He was fair-haired and plump and dressed in very fine clothes. He seemed to be doing all the talking. In contrast to his finery, the cloaks of the Orcadians were sea- and travel-stained. But Jarl Sigurd still stood proudly with his men around him and his raven banner flying high. Skari could see his father in the huddle around the jarl.

And then someone stepped forward to greet Sigurd. It was a black-haired woman: Queen Kormlada, Sitric's mother. Sigurd was presenting her with something, some gift from the Orkneys, probably a finely carved seal bone, or perhaps something even more valuable, a gold or silver ring. Skari squinted, trying to see her clearly. He had heard the stories of her great beauty. He stared. She is old, he thought, even from here you can see the wrinkles on her face, and she is beautiful, but her face – it's a face that's not kind, but fierce and hard. They said she had magical powers, and that she had used them to marry a whole series of kings, including Sitric's father. And now she had promised herself to Jarl Sigurd if he was victorious in the battle against Brian and Malachy.

Old One-Eye grabbed Skari's arm and whispered in his ear. 'So, it will be a great feast tonight. Did you see the tall man with the reddish hair? That's Mael Mordha, King of Leinster, Kormlada's brother and the reason all this started. 'Tis said he was insulted in Brian's court and that the queen worked on him to make him defy Brian. She's a dangerous woman, that one. It's going to be interesting to see how she plays it now. She has promised herself to the Lord of Man, Brodir, as well as Sigurd, if they win the war. So there's trouble ahead, even if we are victorious over Brian. And she's already been married to Brian himself and to the King of Meath! She could always twist men around her little finger. Not just because of her beauty, but because she can charm the birds from the trees – and then rip their little throats open like a cat. She loves power and her greatest power is getting everyone – men, women, children – to do exactly as she wants. That's her way.'

Skari's father, Ragnall, joined them, watching thoughtfully as the group entered the city. 'You're right, Hravn,' he said, 'it's a tangle. And where there is a tangle Kormlada is always in the middle of it, weaving her plots and trapping men in them ...'

The three of them stood looking on as the nobles were led towards the palace. Politics are complicated, thought Skari. Complicated and boring. But at least politics had brought him on this adventure. Skari's father had not been happy about this plan to fight the Irish. He preferred, these days, to stay on their lands and farm them, or fish the waters close to the Birsay coast. 'My gold is in the corn, now, and the only silver I want is the shoals of mackerel around Birsay,' he said to Skari. 'But I must go with my lord, Jarl

Sigurd. That is where my duty lies.'

Skari, full of excitement at the prospect of battle, let out a whoop of joy, and his father continued, 'There's no cause to rejoice, Skari, though I know you're keen to test yourself in battle. War is not beautiful or noble; it's a mean, dirty business. There are times when we have to fight, to protect ourselves. But this is not one of them: this is a war of politics and confusion, and men grasping at power. I wish we did not have to go.'

But Ragnall was one of Jarl Sigurd's most trusted advisors. Skari had hardly seen him during the voyage from Orkney, because he had been made one of Sigurd's personal bodyguards. He was called Ragnall the Wise by the men of Orkney. The Norse liked nicknames, not all of them complimentary: for every Snorri the Stalwart there was a Staari the Skinflint, for every Beorn the Brave there was a Fasti the Flatnosed. Hermund and Skari had often made up names for their less than favourite people. These had included Harald the Hairypants, Ulrika the Unmentionable, Freya the Flatulent, Loki the Lousy and Sven the Smelly.

'Do you have to go back to the jarl straight away?' Skari tried to keep his voice from sounding pleading. It had been a long, lonely voyage.

'Aye, I must get back. There is to be a council meeting now. But you go on, boy; take a look at the city. Be sure come back to the ship before dark. Brodir of Man and his men have already arrived and they are a violent lot, always looking for a fight. Avoid them all you can, especially Brodir himself. He's an ugly customer. Even his own brother, Ospak, has refused to have anything to do with him. Gone over to the Irish, they say. Ah, it's an ugly fight when brother fights brother.'

CHAPTER 5

MEETING IN THE MARKETPLACE

Dublin is like any town, thought Skari, as he wandered through the narrow streets, laden with mud and full of the smell of woodsmoke and pigs. Dirty lanes, low long-houses with women and children peering from the darkness of the doorways. The lane he was following opened out into a marketplace in front of a small stone church. There was no market today, as it was a Sunday, but there were a few stalls laid out along the street. A handful of people were leaving the church. Dublin was now officially a Christian town. Orkney was officially Christian too, but plenty of people still held to the old Norse ways. Skari's father still swore his oaths by Thor and made offerings to Odin before battle. He still called on Frey to make his fields grow good corn and to Freya for the health of the young lambs in their pastures on Birsay.

A scent of something wonderful reached Skari's nostrils and he made his way over to a trestle piled high with spiced cakes. After days of salt fish it was so good to smell something freshly baked. The cakes were marked with what looked like the hammer of Thor, a sign of good Northman baking. And the girl selling them was very pretty. She had long white hair, pale skin and strange silvery eyes set at a slant under dark brows. Her face was serious, almost sad-looking, as she took the cakes from a basket and arranged them on the board.

'How much for these?' he asked, picking one of them up.

The girl smiled. If she had been pretty before, she was dazzling now. 'For you, come to save us from the wild Irish, take what you wish and welcome.'

He smiled his gratitude and bit into the cake. It was delicious. What should he say next? The girl was still busying about with the cakes and pies. She had now been joined by a younger girl, with hair the colour of dark honey and with a friendly, freckled face.

Once again, Skari wished Hermund was with him. He always knew the right thing to say to girls.

'And may I know the name of the maiden that shows such courtesy to a visitor?' Skari asked. He felt a bit stupid being so formal. But that was the way young men of the Orkney court were supposed to speak. And there was somethi about this girl that made him want to impress her.

The girl turned her wonderful silver eyes on him.

'My name is Arna,' she said, 'and I am the daughter of Weland the Smith. This is Elva.'

The younger girl butted in, 'We're sisters.'

Hmm, she's much more ordinary-looking than her big sister, thought Skari, but he smiled politely at both girls.

'And I am Skari, son of Ragnall, Lord of the Broch of Birsay in the Isles of the Orkneys. I've come with Jarl Sigurd's troops to fight against the Irish.'

There was a silence. Skari wondered if he had overdone things by showing off his title. Maybe he should tell them that Birsay was only a little island with a few flocks of sheep and a lot of seagulls? But his familiar shyness was coming over him, leaving him wondering what to say, and, as usual, he tried to make up for it by sounding grown-up. Indeed, it seemed some stupid courtier had got hold of his tongue and he found himself continuing even more pompously, 'It is good to see cakes marked with the sign of Thor. I thought you were all Christians here?'

The younger girl laughed. 'Well, it's the hammer of Thor for the Norse, but if you look at it the other way around it could be the cross of the Christians. That's the way things work in Dublin. My father says there are many ways to look at the same thing! We're doing a great trade in them with the g because it's the feast of Easter next Sunday.'

idn't know quite how to respond to this. He wanted the tall, white-haired girl speak again, so he looked directly and said, 'I thank you for your kindness, but I st insist that the next time I come to your stall I pay for e food. I hope it will be soon. Tell me, what is there to be seen in the city?'

There was a silence. Again, it was the younger one who finally spoke. 'Well, there's the king's palace. And the slave market. And the Thingmote, of course, where the council meets. That's about it, really. Unless you like fish markets and piggeries.'

She seemed about to add something, but she was interrupted by a flurry of skirts and laughter, for someone else had come to the stall. It was Queen Kormlada, with her ladies. And with her too was the man his father had told him to avoid. In fact, Skari had been dying to see him, for he was famous, one of the fiercest warriors in the world.

Brodir of the Isle of Man was tall and heavily built, the skin of his arms almost completely covered in tattoos and arm rings, and a bearskin cloak slung over his shoulders. His black hair was so long he wore it tucked into his belt and his nose was pierced with a silver bone. Some said that Brodir was a true Berserker, and actually turned into a bear when he fought. Others said he called on the power of witches and dark spirits in his battles. Skari looked at him closely. He had a cruel face and a mouth full of black teeth, worn to stumps. Skari had heard it said they had become like that from chewing on his shield, as Berserkers did; though others whispered it was from crunching the bones of enemies when the battle rage was on him.

But Kormlada did not seem to mind his black teeth or the way Brodir held her arm so tightly. She looked at the little group, calmly smiling. Now that he had the full force of her smile directed at him, Skari could understand how all who saw her were bewitched. But her gaze travelled quickly over him and rested on Arna, who was blushing and bowing.

The queen spoke, and her voice was low and gentle. 'Well, my dear Arna, and how are you? By the Morrigan, you are looking prettier than ever. Is she not lovely, Prince Brodir?'

Brodir glanced at Arna and grunted. His attention shifted to Skari. He gave the boy a vicious look and said harshly, 'Bow to the queen, dogchild!'

Skari felt his hand go to his sword but stopped himself just in time; that was what Brodir wanted, a street fight. Skari thought he had never seen anyone who looked less like a great warrior. Brodir was a thug, as tough as nails and with about as much intelligence. His eyes, set close together in his head, were vacant, as if he walked in a dream. There was no way Skari would take on this monster. In any case, it would be very discourteous to start a fight in the streets of Dublin. So he bowed low, and said politely to Kormlada,

'Good day to you, my lady.'

Kormlada's eyes slid over him and she said nothing. But Arna smiled again, and again Skari thought how beautiful she was.

The queen took the girl's hand in hers. 'You must come to see me tomorrow, for we have many things to talk of. Come when the church bells call noon.'

'Yes, my lady.'

Brodir muttered something else in Kormlada's ear, but she shook her head impatiently. Then she was gone in a waft of silk and perfumes, Brodir still clutching her arm.

The little one, Elva, was pulling at her sister's sleeve, whispering furiously, 'You mustn't go, Arna. You mustn't. You know what Father says about her.'

The elder girl shook her sister's hand from her sleeve impatiently. Her voice was shaking when she spoke: 'Father knows nothing about her. You're just jealous because she didn't ask you to come along. I want to go – and anyway, who can refuse a queen?'

'Why don't you want your sister to go?' Skari was curious. There was something dangerous and strange about Kormlada, but also something fascinating. Arna stood silent, her lips pressed together as if determined to say nothing.

Elva said: 'That queen has no good intentions. Her magic is dark and cold, that's what my father says. And she draws young girls into her world, into the darkness and the cold.'

Now Arna turned on her sister: 'You're ridiculous, Elva. She's a great and powerful queen, and deserves our respect, and she knows things others do not even dream of … I *am* going to see her – and you had better say nothing about it or you'll be sorry you opened your big mouth!'

The young girl sighed, looking upset and angry, but said no more. There was an awkward silence. Skari said: 'So that was the mighty Brodir?'

Elva snorted impatiently. 'That thug. The queen leads him around like a pet bear. He's another one she has taken control of!'

But Skari was looking at Arna, thinking she no longer looked so sweet and beautiful. Her eyes seemed blank and lifeless. It's true what they say, thought Skari, Kormlada can bewitch anyone.

The meeting with Brodir had left a sour taste in his mouth. It didn't make him feel good, the thought of going into battle with a brute like that on his side. Full of questions, he bade farewell to the two girls and promised to come back and see them soon.

PART TWO
18–19 APRIL 1014

MANDAGR, TYRSDAGR
DÉ LUAIN, DÉ MÁIRT
MONDAY, TUESDAY

CHAPTER 6

THE MEETING IN THE WOODS

Dara and Niall had spent the morning cutting wood in the underbrush for firewood and shelter. Dara was glad to be doing something. He hated to admit it even to himself, but most of his first day in Kilmainham had been quite boring.

It had begun well, for early in the morning Dara's father had come to him and given him something very precious. It was Ronan's sword, the one their mother had given to her eldest son, beautifully crafted with Norse decorations on the hilt. Cathal's voice was rough with emotion when he handed it to his son.

'You should have this now, Dara. You have proved yourself

worthy to use it. Your mother says it has magical powers. I hope it will protect you when I cannot.'

And later in the morning, King Brian Boru had come to the camp. Dara had been showing the sword to Niall when there was a sudden bustle of activity, and the noise of horse's hooves coming through the forest.

'King Brian must be coming!' whispered Niall. 'That's an honour! We hardly ever see him, with all his war councils – and his prayers ...'

The high king had indeed arrived to greet the warriors from his own lands of Dalcassia and attend mass in the ruined monastery. He rode a great white horse, and he was wearing a cloak of black and white furs. There was a thin gold circlet on his white hair. Brian was tall, with piercing grey eyes and a face that was always, Dara thought, a little sad. The youngest brother of many sons, he had spent his early years in a monastery. When the time had come for him to leave it and fight with his brothers, the Abbot had wept. He could not bear to think that such a clever head might be split open by a Norse axe. But Brian's head had survived, and since he had become high king twelve years ago, he had worked hard at rebuilding the monasteries and libraries that the Norse had raided and robbed.

King Brian of the Tributes was old now, aged over seventy, but he had not lost any of his majesty or his power. Or his graciousness. He dismounted and greeted the men who had come from the south-west warmly. When he saw Dara, he placed his hand gently on his head, giving him his blessing.

Smiling down at him he said: 'Ah, it is good to see you. You are the son of Cathal, and you are my grandson's friend, aren't you?'

Dara bowed lower, glad that his face was hidden from the king. It had been Ronan who had been Turlough's real friend, as he had been the same age as Turlough. He, Dara, had just hung around with them, wanting to be like his older brother and the young prince, but never quite fast enough to catch up with them, never quite skilful enough to take part in their sword fights. Since Ronan's death Turlough had been very kind to him. Yet, somehow, it hadn't helped. Every time he saw Turlough he just missed his brother more.

The king continued, raising his voice to address everyone: 'I thank you for coming to fight with me against our enemies. Rest well while you can, in this peaceful place, for the battle will come soon enough and you will need all your strength then. Rest in the knowledge that we must be victors in this fight, for the Lord is on our side. This is the last battle, the one that will end all battles, making Ireland strong and peaceful under my kingship.'

Rest? thought Dara. He had no intention of taking the king's advice, but he found out he had no choice. The bell from the monastery church had called everyone to attend the Palm Sunday mass, a service that seemed to go on forever.

Sitting on the broken wall, with the priest going on about how all men were brothers in the Lord, Dara felt sleepy and restless. The only diversion was a baby fox that peered out at him from a patch of young ferns. As the chanting continued, and the fox, becoming as bored as Dara, disappeared back into the undergrowth, he began to feel that he could not sit still for even one more moment. He fidgeted in his seat, then caught his father's stern glance. Dara sighed and sat still. His father was strict and King Brian was stricter. Sunday was for religious services, and a day when only essential duties were carried out.

Which, of course, left a lot of work to be done on Monday, as Niall pointed out while they worked their way through a pile of logs. His thoughts still on the battle, Dara jumped as the axe Niall was using missed his foot by inches. Niall, clumsy as ever, had struck wildly at the log they were chopping.

'Watch it, will you!' Dara shouted crossly. 'You're more dangerous than a Norse warrior with that axe!'

Niall was unperturbed; he was used to being teased about his clumsiness. 'Oh look, we've disturbed some rabbits!' he said. They looked on as the young ones raced wildly from their nest. They were a very pale colour, almost white, and Dara suddenly thought of the white animal he had seen in the moonlight. He said to Niall, 'Have there been any stories of a strange white animal being seen around the camp?'

Niall grimaced. 'Nobody ever tells us boys anything! But it's funny you should ask. I haven't seen anything, but I did overhear some of the soldiers talk about being woken in the dark and seeing something white disappear into the trees. Probably just a cat or something. These woods are a bit strange – though not as strange as the ones to the north of the river; they're something else altogether. Remember I told you about them? Where the Norse used to worship their heathen gods, Thor and Odin and the rest of the pagan demons? Those woods are really scary. They used to keep their holy relics there – the Ring of Tomar and the Sword of Carlus.'

'What are they?'

'Like I said, they were special to the Norsemen. Especially the Ring of Tomar – it was a huge arm-ring attached to their altar, and the Norse swore their oaths on it. It was said to have magical powers.'

'So does Malachy have them now up in Meath? Will he have that magical sword and ring when he comes to help us in the battle?'

Niall shook his head. 'Nobody knows what happened to either the sword or the ring. The Norse are mad to get them back, they say. But even if they're gone, there's something weird about those woods. I'm glad we're not camping there. It's bad enough being bored. I don't want to be haunted!'

Turlough joined them. 'Would you two like to take a

break from being woodcutters and come along with me on a little scouting trip?' he asked, the glint of adventure in his eye. 'We're going to go east through the woods to see how close we can get to the walls of Dublin. There are patrols on the walls but we might be able to get near enough to hear what the sentries are saying. Cormac speaks Norse and he'll translate for us. King Brian wants to know what the news is since the ships of Sigurd and Brodir arrived in the harbour.'

Delighted with the idea of a scouting party, Dara and Niall flung down their axes. They made their way silently – or not so silently in Niall's case – down the course of the little river, through the woods that sheltered the narrow valley. It was hard going, with a lot of wading in the water in order to make progress. Then the Camac swerved north towards the Liffey, close to the walls of the city.

Suddenly Cormac stopped. 'Hsst – there's something – there!'

There was a noise of crashing through the undergrowth. It could have been a large deer, even a boar – but it wasn't. It was men, men with no skill for travelling quietly through woods.

A spear zinged past Dara's cheek, missing him by a hair's breadth. They had been spotted by a party of Norse soldiers. Then there was shouting and more crashing through the trees. Bodies came rushing at them through the undergrowth. Dara found himself on the ground, a Norse soldier on his back, pushing him, face first, into the ground. He spluttered, his mouth filled with dead leaves and clay. This made him furious, and with a savage twist, he managed to turn and get himself face to face with the soldier who had jumped him. He realised that it was a boy, perhaps only a few years older than himself, and this made him even more determined to get him off him and at his mercy. He could not get at his sword, but his knife was out. His arm was trapped by the boy's body. Pushing as hard as he could, he managed to turn the blade up into the leather trousers the Norse boy was wearing and felt it dig into the skin of his attacker's leg. His stomach suddenly upended: it was the first time he had cut into human flesh and the feeling was sickening. For the first time he looked up into the face of the boy above him. The boy had not cried out but was gasping with the pain as Dara's knife cut deeper into his flesh.

Through the crazy mix of emotions he was feeling – fear and rage and disgust – Dara caught his breath in astonishment. The eyes looking into his through the mask of the leather helmet might as well have been his own.

There was a rushing noise. Dara had a sense of white wings beating his face, feathers filling his mouth, blinding his eyes. And then, after the whiteness, everything suddenly went black.

When Dara came to, Niall was trying to force some water into his mouth. Most of it, icy cold, went over his face and chest, and he pushed his friend away, gasping and cursing.

'No need to drown me!' He finally managed to get the words out.

Turlough, who was holding Dara's shoulders upright, replied, 'It's not drowning you need to worry about! You must have got some blow there, boyo,' he said, 'but you did manage to make sure your Norseman didn't get away.'

'What? The boy who took me down?'

'Yes, his leg has quite a cut in it, and though he took flight we followed him through the trees and caught him. He's the only one we managed to capture. We might be able to get some information out of him. And you? Are you able to get up?'

Though his head was still spinning, Dara nodded. But as he pulled himself up he felt the gorge rise to his throat. He was still not sure what had happened during the fight with the Norse boy. The whiteness around him had been terrible, and he still felt its suffocating blindness. He took a little more water and managed to stand up, though every bone in his body ached. He looked around the clearing: there were white feathers and fur scattered all over the green grass.

'What happened here?' he asked. 'I remember wings and feathers and whiteness like snow.'

'Must have been when you went out for the count,'

said Turlough. 'There were no birds around, only bloody Norsemen.'

As he went with Turlough to where the prisoner was trussed under a huge beech tree, Dara swore that he would get his revenge on the Norse boy. He should have managed to finish him off during the tussle. But when he saw the boy his anger faded. He had only glimpsed the Norse boy's face for a second and it had been partly hidden by the boy's helmet. Now he could see the black hair that flowed from under it, and that the boy was tall and skinny, and dressed in leathers and furs. He had had his leg wound covered with moss and roughly bound to stop the bleeding, and was slumped as if he had not an ounce of energy left in his body. Now he was not just the enemy. Now he was a real person.

And the question was – what was to be done with their captive?

'We could try and get some information out of him,' said Niall.

'To be honest, I don't know how much he'll be able to help us. He's hardly more than a child. Maybe we should just kill him?' suggested Turlough.

Dara went over to the boy and poked his leg with his toe. 'Do you speak Gaelic?' He asked.

The boy replied: 'And what's it to you, Irish scum, if I do?' He spoke in heavily accented Gaelic.

Dara poked at him a bit harder. 'Only that we have captured you. And are deciding whether to kill you outright or keep you to sell as a slave. So which would you prefer? And where are you from? Whose army are you part of?'

For some reason it seemed important to know where the boy was from. He certainly wasn't Dublin Norse.

Suddenly the boy held his head up proudly.

'I am Skari, son of Ragnall, son of Ar, son of Thorstein. I am of Orkney, of the army of Sigurd the Brave, Lord of the Raven Banner. And we are here to take Dublin for our people, and make you Irish run back to your bog holes in the west.'

The boy's voice was faint but his words were clear. Despite his anger at his words, Dara could not help but feel a little bit of admiration for his courage.

Turlough, beside him, laughed mockingly. 'Brave words, indeed! Let's see the face that lies under the helmet of this firebrand!'

The boy tried to resist as Turlough pulled at the helmet, but he was too weak. Dara stared and Turlough let out a long whistle as the helmet was taken from Skari's head. 'Dara, look at his face! Look at the cleft in his chin. Look at his long nose and his sticking out ears! And his eyes! His eyes are the exact same as yours – one blue, one green! Apart from the colour of his hair and the fact that he's a couple of years older than you, this boy could be your twin!'

CHAPTER 7

IN THE CITY OF DUBLIN

'I wonder will that boy from the Orkneys come back today,' said Elva, as the two girls set up the stall and laid out the cakes their mother had baked that morning. 'You certainly made an impression on him.'

Elva tried to keep the slight note of envy out of her voice. The boy had been nice. He somehow reminded her of the younger one she had met while following Arna – though that boy had been standing in the shadows and it had been hard to see his face, and his hair had been red, not black like that of the Norse boy. But his face had looked just the same. It was odd that they should look so alike.

In reply to Elva, Arna shrugged and looked disdainful.

That, thought Elva, was one of the hardest things about living with Arna during these last few weeks. She never seemed to care about anything. Her father had told Elva that it was just Arna's age, but Elva could not understand how her sister could have changed so much. It reminded Elva of the early days, when she had arrived in Weland's house with her mother. Arna had been so quiet and distant then. Elva had thought she was the most beautiful girl she had ever seen, with her white hair and her wonderful eyes. She had worshipped her, followed her around all the time. Arna had just ignored her, as if she was a somewhat annoying puppy. That had been hard to take, even harder than if Arna had actually been mean to her, so Elva had done more and more things to try to get her attention, borrowing her comb and her cloak, even hiding her mirror. Then one day her mother had taken her to one side and told her that all this must stop.

'You must stop pestering her, Elva. I find Arna difficult too sometimes, I must admit,' she told Elva. 'But she has no mother and I know that makes her really sad. And I think she's a little bit jealous that her father has us now, as well as her.'

'But I have to share *you* with Weland and Arna,' said Elva indignantly. 'And I don't mind it. It's nice to have a father now, and Arna should be happy she has a mother again.'

Her mother sighed. 'I'm afraid it sometimes doesn't work out as easily as that,' she said. Then she hugged Elva tightly.

'Arna may never feel that I am a mother to her, and that is her right. I just wish she could love me a little more. But I'm really happy that you feel that way about your new family. Just be careful with Arna, don't cling to her like ivy and don't look for attention from her all the time. Maybe that will make her pay more attention to you!'

So that was what Elva had tried; and as time went on she made her own friends in the city of Dublin and minded less and less that Arna ignored her. Arna, on the other hand, made no friends at all and didn't seem to want any. And finally, Arna had thawed out. She had been kinder to Elva, letting her comb and plait her hair, talking to her, even giving her little gifts – a ring, a toy. She sometimes even told her secrets, like how her real mother came to her in her dreams and told her stories of the far north, where the whole world was covered in snow and ice. She sang her the songs her mother had sung to her as a baby, beautiful songs. She told her stories about flying over that landscape, free as a bird and wild as a wolf. And Elva discovered that Arna could be very good company – clever and funny, with a tongue that was sometimes cutting but always witty. When people mocked Elva for being half-Irish, Arna would come back with retorts that stopped them in their tracks. She had once asked Beorn, the very worst of the mockers, if *his* grandfather had been a mackerel.

But during the last few months, things had changed again. The trouble started when Arna began to visit Queen

Kormlada in the palace. Since then, Arna started to pay more attention to Elva, but not in a good way. She seemed to take delight in teasing her, driving her into a temper with catty little comments that made Elva fly off the handle. Then Arna would say that it was all a joke, and she didn't know why Elva got so upset. She always seemed to know the one thing to say that would set Elva's temper off. Make her shout and stamp, so that even while she did it, she felt ashamed of herself. Then Arna would smile sweetly at their parents and repeat what she had said to Elva, which somehow no longer seemed so terrible. So Elva would be the one to get into trouble.

Now, as she rearranged the buns on the trestle, Arna smiled and said, 'Just so you know, you can have the Norse boy if you want, I'm certainly not interested.'

Elva blushed furiously. 'I don't know what you're talking about. I just said he seemed to like you, that's all.'

Arna laughed mockingly. 'Oh, don't get so upset, little baby. Why don't you mind the stall while I go and have a look around the market. Maybe your Orkney friend will show up. I won't be long.'

Elva knew there was no point in arguing as Arna always did exactly as she wanted. So she nodded, and Arna grabbed her cloak and ran away swiftly, but not, Elva noticed, into the market. More like towards the palace. The bells rang out from St Olaf's to mark noon and Elva knew she had been right. Arna was going to see Kormlada.

It was evening before her sister came back and Elva had long ago sold the last of the sweet cakes that their mother had baked. She could not take down the trestle or carry the baskets on her own, so she had been stuck waiting in the chill of the evening, watching the other market sellers drift home to warm fires and tasty dinners. By now soldiers from the Norse ships wandered the streets in the twilight, some of them full of ale and looking for a fight. Elva was cold and hungry and miserable and she knew they would both be in trouble when they got home. They were not supposed to stay out so late.

'Where did you go?' she asked furiously, almost in tears with anger. 'I bet you went to see Kormlada, even though you're not supposed to. It wasn't fair to leave me here so long all by myself.'

Then she noticed how strange her sister was looking, her eyes like dark pools in a face that was whiter than snow. 'What is it, Arna?' she asked. 'Did something happen to you?' She gasped when she saw blood on Arna's shoulder. 'Did somebody hurt you?'

Arna shook her head. Her whole body was shaking, but when Elva tried to hug her to give her some comfort, she pulled away and said coldly, 'Come on, we must get home. For the love of Thor, hurry up, we're late already.'

The unfairness of this took Elva's breath away. Whose fault

was it that they were late? But she said nothing. Silently, the two girls dismantled the trestle and loaded up everything for the short trip back home.

When they reached the door, Elva opened it cautiously. She knew there was going to be trouble. But she also knew that there was no point telling her parents that it been Arna who kept them late. They wouldn't listen to her, and Arna would only make her suffer for it later.

But as it turned out, she did not need to worry about punishment from her parents. They were far too busy with the arrival of someone else in the house, someone who needed nursing and care. For there in the hall, lying by the fire with her mother tending to what looked like a knife jab on his leg was the Norse boy who had bought their cakes the day before.

'Look what I found at the gates of the city, escaped from the wild Irish and needing your mother's balms for his wound!' Her father was smiling. 'I believe you have met already. It's a young soldier from the Orkneys. His name is Skari.'

CHAPTER 8

AROUND THE FIRE

Skari could still hardly believe his luck. To have been let free by the Irish! He had been sure he was going to face death, or, at best, life as a slave to some bogger of a chieftain. But when he took off his helmet, the Irish stood around him, staring and pointing and muttering softly about how like he was to the boy who had knifed him. He could see for himself that Dara – that seemed to be the boy's name – was indeed very like him. And he had two mismatched eyes – something Skari had always thought was unique to himself. Maybe they thought this was some kind of sign. Well, thought Skari, it was just a pity his look-alike hadn't realised that before he stuck his knife in Skari's leg!

It was only a flesh wound, but the pain was still very bad. Skari reckoned he must have fainted because of it, for he could remember very little before waking up, trussed up like a hen against the tree. All that was left was a vague memory of something white – was it fur, or was it feathers? – brushing against him. The soft whiteness had reminded him of snow. But whatever had happened, now he lay helpless while the Irish poked and prodded him and asked him questions about his mother.

They forced something foul-tasting down his throat and the young chief of the party said to the tall bearded man, 'What is it, Cormac? Do you think biting your thumb is going to give you Fionn's knowledge?'

The tall man shook himself and stopped biting his thumbnail. 'No, but I'll tell you one thing; we can't kill this lad. And we are not bringing him back to Brian's camp either, he'd cause too much upset there, especially to Dara's father. We can't leave him here, the wolves and whatever else is in these woods would get him. We'll take him as close as we can to the walls of Dublin and sentries will be sure to find him there. Now, lad, on your feet and get moving; nobody's going to carry you.'

The young chief stared at Skari, hard. So did the boy, Dara.

Then the chief said, 'Very well. It would break my heart, in any case, to kill anyone who looked so like Dara – or Ronan. We'll do as you say, Cormac. Come on – Skari – is that your name? You won't have to go far.'

That's just as well, thought Skari, as he stumbled along,

his hands bound by a rope. He kept half-tripping in the undergrowth. He decided that he did not like being in these woods. Even as part of the patrol he had been fearful as they'd made their way into the darkness, imagining every branch that brushed against him an enemy's sword or the tickle of a dagger point against the back of his neck. He had also been aware that they were making a noise like boars crashing through the undergrowth – half of the Irish camp must have heard them. He was not used to moving in the forest. In the Orkneys, there were wide green hills stretching down to the waves, so that you could see all around you. And endless, shining seas that protected his people against every invader.

When they reached the town wall, he collapsed against it. He could not have staggered another step, his leg ached so much and he felt so weak.

'Not a word out of your mouth until the sun has risen above that pine tree,' said the tall man. 'Or we'll be back to slit your throat.'

But even if he had wanted to, Skari hadn't had the strength to call out. He felt as if all his energy had been drained from him. He lay by the wall and watched the small birds hop through the branches of the wood that grew so close against it. He could hear the sound of the river. He must have fallen into a doze for when he woke the wood was chilled with evening. He himself felt warm, as if he had been covered with a cloak. As he peered into the darkening wood, he thought he could see something white move through the trees. The he realised that he could hear men's voices. He listened hard. They were speaking Norse. A patrol was coming along the walls. He tried to call out but only a faint sound came from his parched throat. However, he could hear the men stop in their tracks.

One of them said, 'Did you hear something?'

''Twas nothing, just some bird or animal.'

Skari tried to call again. If he was not discovered he would spend the night out here, and he might not survive it … apart from the fact that his wound had started to bleed again, there was a strange feeling in this wood. Faint and sick, Skari again half-thought he saw something out of the corner of his eye ... something white. But now the men were coming down the bank.

One of them, a huge man with a red beard, was saying, 'I knew I heard something. Why, it's a lad, and one of ours by the look of his gear. Wounded, though, look at his leg.'

The other came close and peered at him. 'Who are you, boy, and what are you doing here?'

'I am Skari, Ragnall of Orkney's son. I was with Olaf, Son of Bjorg's patrol.' He took a breath and continued, 'We came upon Brian's men this morning in the wood. We were too few – I was wounded but for some reason the Irish didn't kill me. I don't know why. They brought me here. I … Did the others get back safe?' Exhausted from speaking, Skari stopped. He hadn't the energy to try to start to explain about his look-alike Irish attacker.

The big, red-haired man hoisted him up over his shoulder. 'I don't know about the others in the patrol, but you can't stay here, that's for sure. Let's bring you back into the town. Your father is probably still with the other lords, so for the moment I'll take you to my house so we can bind that wound properly. It has a nasty look to it and my wife has some skill in healing. We must get you out of this cold.' He shivered, then continued, 'I am Weland, the smith, by the way. Ralf, you can finish the round on you own, can't you?' Ralf nodded. 'It's only few minutes before the new watch starts anyway. See you tomorrow, then.' They two men slapped each other on the shoulder and parted ways.

Skari wondered if his father would have heard about the attack on the patrol. He said to Weland, 'Don't you think I should go straight back to the ships? My father may be worried about me.'

'I'll send one of the boys from the forge with a message. Don't worry about that – that wound needs to be cleaned and bandaged properly. And if you come back with me you can meet my daughters and have some good hot food. My wife is the best cook in Dublin.'

'There must be great cooks in Dublin, then,' said Skari, in a brave attempt to be courteous to his host. 'I already had some wonderful spiced buns.'

'Indeed? And who did you buy them from?'

'Two girls in the market.'

'Then you have met my daughters already. And tasted my wife's cooking!'

When they arrived at the longhouse, Birgit, Weland's wife, immediately took over, and Skari spent a few painful minutes having his wound washed and bound. But the ointment Birgit smeared on it worked straight away. After a short while Skari was able to walk gingerly on his wounded leg. Birgit, however, told him to sit himself down and stay still, and sent the maid, Astrid, to bring him some soup and oatmeal bread.

'That's just to warm you up,' said Birgit. 'We'll eat supper when the girls come in – though they should be here already. I wonder what has them so late?'

Birgit didn't wait for an answer. She hardly paused for breath as she worked, but that didn't stop her being a whirlwind of efficiency. She looked very like Elva, Skari thought, except that her hair was a darker brown. Her eyes were like her daughter's, the colour of amber. She didn't look a bit like Arna – where *did* that girl get her pale hair and strange eyes from?

When the two girls finally did arrive, he got a shy smile from Elva and one of those piercing looks from Arna. Astrid and Birgit served up dinner to them all. It was delicious food, with meat as well as onions and leeks in the stew. Around the fire, it was warm and cosy. Skari, looking around him, thought that everyone seemed comfortable and happy together. He suddenly felt very lonely, remembering his own home, missing his sister and his stepmother. Ingrid would have loved the warm, colourful rugs like the one thrown over him, and the shining pewter and finely carved bone spoons. But it was more than the furs and the fire that made Skari feel warm. It was the way everyone sat together – Weland's two helpers from the workshop, Astrid and the family, and the dogs and cats sitting close by, waiting patiently for titbits; everyone warmed by the glow of the fire, doubly safe within the walls of the house and the outer walls of the city.

But now the dishes were being taken away and they sat around the fire, Pingin curled in Elva's lap and Rolf with his head on Arna's knee. She scratched him absently behind the ears, gazing into the fire. Weland was talking, asking Skari to tell him a little about himself.

Elva cut in excitedly, 'But let him tell us about the battle he was in today first!'

Skari couldn't help smiling. 'It really wasn't much of a battle; we just ambushed some Irish outside the walls. I don't remember a lot before I was wounded and blacked out. It was so weird; there was this feeling of something soft and cold covering me. Like snow.'

Astrid said, 'Oh, we had terrible snow in Dublin last winter. It was really terrible. Is it snowy all winter where you live?'

Skari shook his head. 'No. Not usually. But this year was

strange. We are used to the wind where I'm from, but the wind that came last autumn was the worst ever – so bitter and cold and harsh. Then the snow came. At the beginning it seemed harmless, beautiful even, but it kept on falling and falling and falling. In the end we could hardly leave the house. Len, one of my father's friends, died trying to save his sheep from a snowdrift. And another man lost his way in a blizzard and died only a few yards from his house.'

Arna spoke, her voice dreamy, 'But snow is so beautiful. It makes everything bright and pure. When we had snow here, it covered all the dirt of the city. The way the brightness reflected back from it made the darkest days of winter full of light.' Her voice changed, became rougher. Skari wondered if she was trying to hold back tears. 'But then it stopped, and everything went back to its usual dirty self.'

Astrid giggled. 'Oh, we couldn't get Arna to come in out of the snow while it lasted! But I didn't like it, I hated the cold–'

Elva said impatiently: 'Never mind the snow … tell us what happened, Skari, when you were attacked.'

'Well, in fact, we attacked them first. But there were three of us and four of them. Though two were only boys, one younger than me. I think his name was Dara – he was the one who gave me the cut.'

'Dara? What did he look like?' Elva sounded even more excited.

'That's the strange thing, he looked a lot like me, and that's why they let me go, I think.'

'What? Do you have relatives among the Irish?'

'I have never heard of any, though I suppose it might be possible. My father is pure Orkney, one of Earl Sigurd's men: he has fought with him for many years. But my mother was an Irish slave; she died after I was born. I don't remember her.'

'That's so sad,' said Birgit, who was mending a tear in Elva's saffron cloak as she listened.

Skari shrugged. He had not really missed having his birth mother around. 'My stepmother, Ingrid, has been like a mother to be. And I have a little sister, Gudrun.'

'That's like Arna; her mother has left us too. But now she has a mother in Birgit!' Weland spoke genially.

Arna said nothing, staring into the fire, as if she could still see the snow in the flames.

So that was it, thought Skari. That's why she doesn't look like Birgit.

'And little Elva's father is dead too. He was Norse. We have lots of people in Dublin who are a mixture of Norse and Irish,' said Weland. 'There's a lot of marrying between the two races – even the king has an Irish wife!'

Birgit nodded. 'Yes, strange as it sounds, Sitric's wife is one of Brian Boru's daughters. But at least she doesn't get involved in politics, not like that other one, Kormlada.'

Skari gave a quick look at Arna, and saw her face stiffen. 'I saw the queen yesterday' he said. 'She's very beautiful.'

'Aye, they say dragons and snakes are beautiful too,' said Weland. 'She's beautiful and cruel, with a mind always bent to mischief, and she dabbles in dark magic, to boot. They say that she was behind this latest war, encouraging her brother Mael Mordha to take offence and insult the high king of the Irish. It all started with a row over a game of chess – 'tis a small thing to bring so many young men to their deaths. It was Kormlada's meddling that pushed her brother to defy Brian.' Weland's voice was stern.

But Birgit interrupted, 'Ah, it's too easy to blame a woman for the start of a war. But you know it has been building up for a long time – Mael Mordha of Leinster wants Brian's power, and Sitric does not want Dublin threatened again by the Irish. Nor does he want to pay tribute to either Brian or Malachy of Meath. This is about much more than a chess game. It's about power and land and money, as wars always are.' Birgit sighed and bit off the thread she had been sewing with, then laid the cloak aside. 'Now, enough of politics. It's late and you need your sleep. You can sleep over beside Than and Wendel there' – she pointed to where Weland's apprentices slept – 'and let us hope that their snoring doesn't keep you awake.'

But Skari wanted to hear more about Kormlada. 'But the queen – can she really do magic? Is it true that she can cast spells on people to make them do what she wants?'

It was Weland who answered him. Skari noticed that he was crouched as close as possible to the fire, as if the cold he had mentioned earlier had got into his bones. 'It's hard to know if what she does to men is magic or just good lying. Making them all believe what she wants. Like she promised Brodir of Man *and* your leader, Jarl Sigurd, that she would marry them. Though you would think they'd have enough sense to realise that a marriage to Kormlada doesn't last long. Our own king of Dublin was the only one who didn't divorce her – and that was only because he died before he got the chance!'

'A happy escape, I'd say,' said Birgit, sniffing in a disapproving way. 'And now she wants to get her hands on our Arna. Don't think I haven't heard about you going to her in the palace, girl. You know very well her ways are not of the light. I don't want to hear any more reports of you going there. If I do, you won't be allowed out of the house for a month.'

When Arna spoke, her voice was very cold. 'Has my little sister been sneaking on me?'

Elva broke in, 'That's not fair! I never said a word–'

'No, it wasn't Elva', said Birgit, 'though she should have told us. It was Magrit, the Volva. She saw you with Kormlada. I met her in the marketplace the other day and she told me. Don't look so angry, Arna, you know I'm saying this for your own good.'

Poor Arna, thought Skari. Didn't her parents realise that she was no longer a little child and needed some freedom? Though spending time with Kormlada probably wasn't the best way to spread your wings – the queen seemed to take control over everyone she met. He hoped he would get a chance to talk to Arna, to let her know he knew how she felt. But Arna didn't look at him at all.

Now Birgit continued: 'Enough, let's not be fighting in front of our guest. It's time for all of us to go to sleep. Here, Skari, take one of the furs as well as the blankets. These spring nights are still bitterly cold. I'll have another look at that wound in the morning, though I think it should heal cleanly.'

PART THREE
21–22 APRIL, 1014

ODINSDAGR, THORSDAGR
DÉ CÉADAOIN, DÉARDAOIN
WEDNESDAY, THURSDAY

CHAPTER 9

THE LOCKED CHEST

... Arna has changed herself into a white stoat, with gleaming red eyes ...

... Arna has changed herself into a great white bird, with a blood-covered beak ...

... Arna's wings are flapping over her face, smothering her ...

... and now, as Elva tosses restlessly under the furs of the bed, Arna has become human.

But Elva is no longer safe behind the walls of Dublin. Arna is walking away from her, leaving her alone in a vast snow-covered landscape, a desolate and silent world. Whiteness is stretching away as far as the eye can see. Her sister is wearing a cloak made of white cats' skins, but Elva has no cloak. She is left shivering in her shift, with no boots on, her feet frozen in the snow …

She looks around her and hears a sound – the clack-clack-clack of a bird. It is unlike any she has ever seen – its wings are a mixture of black and white. The bird is fat and shiny and hops towards her, its head on one side, as if about to ask her a question.

She's frightened of it, and when it opens its beak and starts to fly towards her she sees that its eyes are dark red …

Elva woke up with a cry. Blood-red eyes were still looking into hers. They belonged to Arna. Elva's cry was strangled in her throat as Arna put out her hand and clasped her sister around the neck. The red in her sister's eyes faded to silver and Arna gave a strange, quiet laugh, putting her finger to her lips.

Then, quick as a flash, she was gone from the bed, running towards the door of the house. Elva grabbed her cloak and ran after her, but Arna was going too fast. She had already run beyond the turn of the lane. The moon, its silver circle high in the sky, had begun to wane, its bright roundness beginning to rub away. Should she try to follow her sister? But Elva knew that she would never be able catch up, and she stood in the street, shivering and barefoot, until she felt her mother's warm cloak being wrapped around her and heard her voice.

'Come in, child, out of the cold, out of the moonlight,' her mother whispered, leading her back towards the house.

'But what about Arna? Where has she gone?' Elva whispered back.

'Shh, don't wake no-one. Come with me into the forge where it's warm and quiet and I'll tell you. Though I promised Weland I would not. But I reckon if I don't, no-one else will and you may find yourself in danger because of your sister.'

The guard-goose they kept in the forge, Ulla, raised her head from her nest when they entered, and then, when she saw who it was, settled down again without making a sound. Seated beside the fire, with her mother's arm around her, Elva felt safe again. But her mother had a worried, doubtful look on her face when she began to speak.

''Tis all to do with Arna's mother, Weland's first wife,' she explained, 'the beautiful Svanhild. She was a strange one, with great powers, magical powers. Your father loved her dearly, and I think she must have loved him too. She bore him Arna. Then she went away, leaving her baby to be brought up by Weland. That was all of thirteen summers ago. Not a word or a sign of her since. But now something has happened. Something has been woken. I don't know what exactly. I think it has something to do with Queen Kormlada and the magic she's stirring up in this town, calling on old, dark spirits for help in the battle. Or it may be to do with Svanhild herself. Maybe she's calling to her daughter, drawing Arna away from us, across into her world. Her world is not yours or mine.

Elva, listen to me carefully and promise me something: it is a world you must not go close to, for those humans who do make their way there often cannot come back to us. You must promise me that you will not interfere.'

Elva nodded, but she was hardly paying attention to what she was promising. She was intent on trying to puzzle out the mystery. 'But what about Arna? Is she not human?'

'Aye, she's human, and my heart goes out to her, for she is only a child and she's dealing with things no child should have to deal with. She's human because her father is human enough, though a human with special powers himself. What her mother was, I cannot tell you, for I never met her and Weland rarely speaks to me about her. All I know is she sang strange songs to her baby and she hid many strange things in that great chest by the fire. Most of them she took with her, but some she left for Arna to have when she reached her thirteenth birthday.'

'But Arna's birthday is this week! It's on Friday!'

'Indeed it is, and I reckon that's part of the reason why she has been so strange lately.'

'What's in the chest?'

'I don't know. It hasn't been unlocked since the lady Svanhild left. And I think I don't want to know either. I've been dreading the day it's opened these many years. But that's enough of these old stories. Now you must try to sleep. Your sister will return safely – doesn't she always? I know it's worrying, I'm half-mad with worry myself, but when I try to talk to Arna she tells me nothing. I can't get through to her at all.'

'Why has she got like that? Is it Kormlada?'

'It is to do with her. But Arna's own sadness hasn't helped – the wound she has had in her heart since her mother went away has left her open to the poison of Kormlada. But say nothing of this to your father. I think he must be coming down with a sickness – he's shivering all the time. And with the attack on Dublin ahead of us, he has worries enough as it is.' She herself shivered. 'We all have.'

The next morning was rainy and cold. Skari was fetched back to the ships by a messenger from his father, and Elva watched him go, a little sad that they hadn't had a chance to get to know each other better. She might never see him again. Who knew what might happen to him in the battle? She thought of all the soldiers, boys like Skari, boys like Dara, boys only a little older than she was, heading out to war. So many of them would not come back. And who knew what might happen to her own family, if the walls of Dublin fell? All these soldiers, surrounding them on all sides – some of them were meant to be protecting them, it was true, but how much protecting would someone like Brodir do? She sometimes felt as if the city was like a fragile egg held in the palm of a great hand, a hand that might not protect, but close over it and crush it.

But she was given no time to brood. Her mother had a look on her face that Elva knew only too well. It meant that she was determined to keep her daughters busy and out of mischief. She had a long list of chores lined up for both Elva and Arna. But at noon she was called away to a sick neighbour, and the house was left empty and quiet, with just the dim thud of Weland and his apprentices at work in his forge next door coming through the walls.

Elva leant on her broom and looked at the richly carved chest that stood against the end wall of the house. It was the most beautiful piece of furniture the family possessed. The dark wood was covered in carvings of strange animals and birds. There were serpents swallowing their tails, dragons' heads, branches twisting and curling into a pattern that made her dizzy if she tried to follow it with her eyes. Today, it felt as if the dragons' eyes had been watching Elva all day, calling to her, urging her to open the chest. And her mother, in her rush to help her neighbour, had left behind the keys that usually hung safely from her belt. There they were, still stuck in the lock of the chest she had fetched the medicine from. Elva went towards them, hardly daring to breathe. Rolf looked up and barked sharply at her, almost making her jump out of her skin. Her hands were shaking as she took the keys from the medicine chest. What if her mother found her doing this? Or worse, Arna?

She knelt and placed the key in the lock of the carved chest. The lock was stiff, and she had to use her two hands, but finally she felt the key turn. She lifted the lid slowly, half afraid that what was inside might fly out at her, like the black and white bird in her dream.

But nothing did fly out. Not even a moth. Looking down into it was like looking into a deep well, a black pool. At first she thought it was empty. Then she saw there was something buried so far inside that she had to bend halfway into the chest to pull it out. A scent of old rosemary filled her nostrils as she peered into the darkness. Deep in the dark well, something was shining, bright as the full moon.

It was cool in Elva's hand as she pulled it out, a silvery fish coming out of black water. It was a necklace. As she held it up into the light, Elva saw that it was very lovely. It was hinged at the front so it could be opened out, and the hinge was covered with a most beautiful piece of metalwork. It showed a gold and silver scene of a tree, a well, and a bird. The bird was taking flight from the flames that came from the top of the tree. She gazed at it, but although it was beautiful, she found she did not want to hold it too long. The metal was so very cold. She placed it carefully at the edge of the chest, where the metal glinted in the light, a silver eye, watching her.

Looking into the chest again, she realised that there was something else there. Lying at the base was more brightness, something as white as snow. She reached down again. This time there was softness under her fingers, and she pulled out a cloak made from swan's feathers. Elva held it up against her face: it was light and soft as a spring breeze. And underneath it was a pair of boots made from white fur, and a pair of gloves too, of the same soft whiteness. The clasp on the cloak was made of silver and decorated with white stones. There was a scent from it, something Elva did not recognise, which made her feel sleepy and at the same time intensely awake. As if she could see a picture in her head ... now she was looking across a lake at a flock of swans – or was it a group of white-haired girls in swan cloaks? Were they singing, was there music coming across the water, lulling her, calling her ... She opened the cloak gently; it was so beautiful, like a swan's wings. She would just try it on to see how its soft airiness felt around her, enveloping her–

'What are you doing? In the name of Thor, what are you *at*?' Harsh fingers gripped her shoulders and a voice thundered in her ear. Her father was behind her. He spun her around to face him, forcing her to drop the cloak. 'Leave those things be! Do you hear me! Who said you could look in that chest? You little fool, you have no idea what you're meddling with!'

Elva had never seen her father so angry, at least not with

her. His face was crimson and his eyes – even his eyes seemed red, glowing like coals.

'I'm sorry – I just wanted to know ...' Her voice trailed off.

'To know what?'

'About Arna, I wanted to see what her mother left her. I heard it was something special. I'm sorry, I'll put everything back carefully.'

Her father buried his face in his hands. 'It's too late for that, child! Thor curse whoever told you about the chest. Who was it?'

Elva said nothing, but thankfully her father's mind had moved on.

'Why did you suddenly decide to look in the chest now? You know we never open it!' He didn't sound quite so angry now.

'It was only that I've been so worried about Arna. She's been sneaking out every night. I followed her once and she was in the Irish camp, leaning over the sleeping soldiers. She seemed to be still asleep even while she was doing it.'

Her father sighed. He was very pale and his hands were shaking. 'In that case it is, indeed, well too late to keep the chest locked. Oh, my poor Arna! She has probably opened it herself already.'

He picked up the necklace and looked at it closely. When he spoke, there was awe in his voice. 'I had forgotten how beautiful this was. The work of dwarves, or elves perhaps.

Marvellous work.'

'Look how it opens out ...' Elva whispered.

'Aye. Though it's a strange design. That hinge is more like a slave collar than a necklace. But it's neither. It's an arm-ring – big enough for the arm of a great warrior. Or the neck of a young girl. Svanhild and I closed and locked this chest together. It was long before you were born but Svanhild had ... Svanhild was special ... and she knew that what was in the chest might bring danger.'

'Danger to who?'

'Danger to whoever might wear it. And those close to her.' Weland sighed wearily. 'It's a long story, and too sad a tale for someone as young as you are. It goes back to the time the Irish burned and hacked their way through the sacred grove where Thor was worshipped. They have a great hatred of that place; Malachy of Meath attacked it, Brian Boru attacked it ... they did it because it is a place of power, of power that they do not understand. That they don't even want to admit is real.'

'Tomar's Grove? In the wood north of the Liffey?' Elva had heard of the wood and its ruined sanctuary, but had never been there. No-one in Dublin liked to go through that part of the forest.

'Aye, Tomar or Thor's grove. It was the Irish revenge, they say, for the times the Norse had gone viking and burned their churches and monasteries. There was a ring and a sword there, and they were stolen. They say that when the ring and the sword are brought back to the grove, the old gods will wake again and the spirits of the grove will take revenge for the violence done to them. Elva,' he urged, 'say nothing about this to anyone. Not even your mother. She has worries enough as it is. Can I trust you on this?'

Elva nodded dumbly. Here was her father telling her not to tell her mother about the chest. Her mother had said the same to her. Her parents had always seemed so united when there was trouble in the house, working together to make things better. Now they were keeping secrets from each other. Arna – and Kormlada and her black magic – were breaking Elva's family apart, unbinding all the threads of love and loyalty woven by her parents over the years. Both Birgit and Weland had always seemed so at ease with life. Now both were desperately worried. It seemed that even they could not do anything to stop what was happening to Arna. Elva felt something in her chest, a feeling she had not had for years, not since she had come to Weland's house. It was not fear; she had felt fear since then. It was something that chilled her to ice and made her feel as if she could not breathe. It was terror.

CHAPTER 10

TOMAR'S GROVE

As they made their way back to camp, Cormac refused to say any more about the strange boy they had left at the Dublin walls. Dara glanced at him often, but his face was set and hard. Dara knew that Cormac knew something about Skari that he was not telling them. Why did the boy look so much like him, he wondered. He must surely be related to him – but how could an Orkney boy be related to him? How could he have the same mismatched eyes? The only other person that had eyes like his was his mother. Now here was that strangeness again in this Norse boy's face.

And what exactly had happened when he had attacked Skari? Where had that feeling of being suffocated under feathers or fur come from? There had been something white and cold covering his mouth and nose, he was sure of that.

Had it something to do with the white creature he had seen sneak through the camp? He was determined to stay awake tonight and see if it appeared again.

But, as it happened, Dara slept like a log and didn't wake up until the rest of the camp was up and stirring and the sun had already risen over the rim of the trees. His dreams had been deep and, for some reason, when he woke up the world felt brighter. It must have been the draught Cormac had given him before sleep time – he had been sick and anxious all evening, unable to eat and trying hard to not feel nauseous every time he thought of the encounter with the Norse boy. His first real battle; surely he should have felt wonderful? But he had not felt wonderful. He had felt wretched. His mind kept going back to that awful feeling of his knife slicing through the other boy's flesh. Niall was rabbiting on and on about how next time none of their attackers would get away, but Dara sat silent and half-shivering in the cold, damp dusk of the forest.

His uncle, passing, grasped his shoulder and shook him gently. 'Ah boy, you look chilled to the death. Stay there a moment and I'll get you something to warm you.' He had come back with a beaker filled with a deep red liquid. 'Drink this,' he said. 'It's been a hard day for you.'

'Cormac, will you tell me who that foreigner boy was?' asked Dara.

'I would if I was sure. But it's only a suspicion I have. And even if it's true it is not my story to tell,' said Cormac. 'You will need to ask your father when you see him. He's busy now, over with the men of Meath, but tomorrow you should go to find him and he will tell you what you need to know. The best thing you can do now is sleep. That's what you need most of all.'

And Cormac had sung, then, not a war song but a lament. Although the song was about a battle, it did not celebrate victory but instead told the story of King Sweeney, who had gone mad from the horror he had seen in the fight, and taken to the trees like a bird or a wild animal.

In the morning the men stood around the fires, cups in their hands, chatting. There was a buzz of excitement in the air.

Dara was on his way to look for his father when Turlough came over to him, grinning. 'The Viking ships have left Dublin!' he said.

'What? They're *leaving*? They're not going to fight us?'

Turlough shook his head. 'That's what they want us to think. But they've probably just gone to anchor somewhere on the shore to the north or south of Dublin. Probably the north – the sands are flatter there so it's easier to land. We're not sure whether they're doing it to try to fool us or because of the trouble Brodir's soldiers are causing in Dublin. The word has got through that they're a wild bunch, fighting with everyone and telling mad stories about witches and demons. We're sending out scouting parties to see if we can spot where the ships are lying. Niall has volunteered to come along. Do you want to come too? We can have a look at the main army camp north of the Liffey while we're at it. Or did you have enough excitement yesterday?'

There was friendly mockery in Turlough's eyes. Dara put out of his mind the memory of yesterday's horror. There was no way he was going to let Turlough think that yesterday had been too much for him. 'Of course I do! Just let me get my stuff.'

Within a few minutes Turlough's party had moved north across the river and through the trees that stretched far beyond the city of Dublin.

'We're getting close to Tomar's Wood,' said Turlough, 'where the heathens used to worship their gods – Thor and Odin and all those devils. 'Tis said they used to hang bodies from the trees and leave them to the birds to strip off the flesh as part of their horrible sacrifices.'

Niall was starting to look a little green; more or less the way Dara was starting to feel.

'Thor is their god of thunder, isn't he?' Dara asked.

'Yes. And he's the one most of the Dubliners worship. The Viking nobles call themselves the soldiers of Thor. His symbol is a hammer.'

'But I thought the Norse were Christians now?'

'Some of them are Christians; the king himself is one. But scratch the surface of a Norseman and you'll find a pagan, my dad says. Most of them are a bit of both! Lots of them have a saying: Christ on the land, but Thor on the water ... And some of them have turned back to the ways of their fathers. Have you seen Prince Ospak yet? His brother, Brodir of Man, is one of those. He's in league with demons and has magical powers. Wherever he gets it from, he's one of the strongest, most savage warriors on the Norse side! I'm going to fight him *and* the King of Leinster, when we go to battle!'

'Me too!' said Niall.

'Well, you'd better learn to hold your sword properly so!' said Dara crossly. 'You nearly stuck it into my leg a minute ago.'

As they travelled through the wood, the trek became harder. There were tall old trees with heavy, low-hanging branches that blocked their way. But even worse was the undergrowth of twisted saplings and bushes, brambles and tall nettles, newly sprung up in the warmth and light of late April. The tangle was made up of different kinds of trees – willow and alder, hazel, birch and green, thorny holly. Dara didn't mind the hard going; he loved the woods, especially at this time of year. There were so many greens, from the dark moss that felt so soft under his hand to the pale, unfurling beech leaves. The young oaks glowed, pale gold, their leaves the very last to open out. He didn't even care when they had to make their way through the marshy patches, where the thin streams of silver were surrounded by squelching black mud that sucked them down into it, almost as far as their knees.

But then the forest changed. First there was the silence. The birds had stopped singing. Then there was the smell, not the fresh smell of growth and warm earth that filled the rest of the forest, but a smell like iron and blood that caught in their throats and made them choke. They had come to a place of horror. The sky darkened and a wind rose up, biting their skin. Here, the trees had been hacked at, their branches savagely lopped off. Some had been burnt, and were no more than blackened stumps. The ground was covered with the leafless branches. It was a ruined, ravaged place, a place that made Dara think of a battlefield covered in mutilated bodies.

'Where are we?' asked Dara, although he had a good idea that he already knew.

'This is the grove,' said Turlough, his voice a whisper. 'This is where they kept the Sword of Carlus and the Ring of Tomar. Their lost treasures. This is where they worshipped their gods.'

Dara's head was spinning. The light through the trees was so bright it dazzled him; and he could hear a murmuring, a buzzing in the silence that hung so heavily on the grove.

The sword that Dara carried, Ronan's sword, drawn and

ready for action, suddenly felt like fire in his hand. The buzzing in his head got worse and he knew he was going to fall. He put out a hand against as tree trunk and leapt back with a cry – it felt like flame against his skin.

'What's wrong?' Turlough had stopped the party.

Dara struggled to keep his head clear. He knew he couldn't stay in this place. He staggered forward, and the ground gave way beneath him. He felt a crunch and he looked down, then jerked back his foot in horror. He had stepped into a nest of … something … on the ground. A nest. A nest that had been full of eggs, but now he had broken them. And what came oozing from the shells was not the yolk and white of normal eggs, but a grey, sticky mucus that he frantically tried to brush off his foot with some ferns.

He felt sick to his stomach now, but said stoutly, 'I'll be fine. Let's just get away from here. I don't like this place.'

With Niall and Turlough's help, he made his way over the fallen branches which caught at his feet. The branches from above him were tightly interlaced, like arms in a crazy dance or a web made by a mad spider, catching at him, trying to poke out his eyes. He still couldn't see clearly. But there seemed to be people around him, not the scouting party but tall men with long white hair and women carrying spindles … all of them were pale, with fierce, sad eyes. And all of them were murmuring, chanting strange words that struck like hammers inside his head. Cold seemed to seep from them, making him shake and shiver so that he could hardly put one foot in front of the other. Making him want to grasp at the trees to steady himself ... but the trees were on fire ...

'Come on, Dara, don't give up, we'll get you through.' Turlough's voice sounded wonderfully normal and human.

And finally they did reach the other side of the grove. They crossed out of the ring of trees, back into the darkness of the forest. To Dara it was like diving into water, after having been burnt in the flame and frozen in the cold. The feeling of dizziness passed, the white-faced people disappeared. But now he couldn't go any further and collapsed under an oak tree.

Turlough slid down beside him. 'What was all that about, Dara?' he asked.

Dara shook his head. 'I don't have a clue. It was as if there was something weird there, trying to keep me with it. As if it wanted something from me.' He touched the blade of his sword. It was as cool as water. 'Whatever it was, I'm glad it's over!' He put as much courage as he could into his voice. 'I'm ready to go on now.'

They continued on through the trees until they could see light ahead. They had reached the grey line of the sea.

'We are at the Bull's Meadow,' said Turlough. 'That's the island ahead of us. But look – look there on the shore – far out on the sands. It's the Viking fleet. Look at those dragon-headed prows! There's probably more of them behind Howth and the island. There must be hundreds of them!'

CHAPTER 11

MAGIC OR MADNESS?

The boats, beached on the shore of the small island that faced the Bull's Meadow, rocked gently in the wind, a cold wind from the Norse homelands to the north-east. Skari looked towards the woods that lined the coastline. They were beautiful woods. They had been sacred woods once, but were desecrated now. Irish soldiers might be skulking in there now, watching them from the cover of the trees. How dare they take over the holy places of the Norse? He tried to make himself feel angry against the Irish: that was the proper way to prepare for battle. Filled with rage against the enemy. That was the Norse way, the Berserker way. Their songs praised those who forgot everything but their anger when they went into battle. That was the way to gain glory. Every soldier had his own method of calling on the gods to give him that kind of mad courage. Some of them drank potions; others danced and chanted themselves into battle fury. Some made sacrifices to Odin for victory and Thor for their safety. Brodir was especially famous for how he could work himself into a rage, with his crazy chanting and dancing. When he was like that no man could stand against him.

But now, looking at the sunset blazing behind the trees, Skari could not feel anger. The landscape was peaceful and beautiful and spoke of the coming of summer and calm blue seas. There was a man ploughing one of the fields at the edge of the bay. In another, some cows stood grazing peacefully, in a field dotted with buttercups. One raised her head and licked the little calf standing close by her. People and beasts who just wanted to get on with their lives. From here, you could not tell if they were Norse or Irish. Skari shook himself. Better not to think too much. That was the best advice around battle time. He decided he would go to find his father.

His wounded leg was still hurting as he walked to his father's tent, but he tried his best not to limp. His father grinned at him.

'So you have been getting yourself into trouble with the Irish, I hear. Sit down. Does your leg still ache?'

Skari shook his head.

'They let you back alive, though? How did that happen?'

Skari shook his head again. 'I don't really know. But it had something to do with the fact that I looked so much like the Irish boy, one of the Dalcassians. It was so strange, Father: he is a couple of years younger than me but he has my face – only he has red-brown hair, not black. His eyes are just the same colours as mine – one blue, one green.'

Skari's father sat down heavily on a stool. His face took on a strange look.

'What was the boy's name and people?'

'He was called Dara. He said he was the son of Cathal of the Dalcais.'

'Did he speak of his mother?'

Skari looked at his father closely. He had shut his eyes, as if afraid to look at his son.

'No.'

'He didn't mention a Lia, of the Clan of the Seahound?'

'No, but what about her? Do you know her?'

His father opened his eyes and sighed. He started to speak, but at that moment there was an interruption. The jarl's messenger entered the tent, his face red from running.

'Ragnall! Jarl Sigurd is looking for you. You must come – now!'

His father stood up, shaking himself like a horse who wants to rid himself of flies. 'No time for any more of this. I must go to Jarl Sigurd's tent; there are plans being made for the battle.'

'But what were you going to tell me?'

'I will tell you all, and tell you soon. But I must go now.'

'Can't I come with you?'

'Come along if you wish, though I doubt they will allow you to stay.'

But when they reached the tents, Jarl Sigurd said: 'Let him stay! How else is he to learn unless by listening to his elders?'

So Skari tried to make himself as small as possible and listened with all his attention while the discussion went on … and on. The war council argued and agreed and then argued again. About how many men the Irish had. About whether the King of Meath would come to fight with Brian. About how the tides would affect the battle. After what seemed like centuries, they finally agreed on a plan. The Norse and Leinstermen would fan out over the sands when the troops met in battle. Mael Mordha would lead one of the battalions against the forces of King Brian; the others would be led by Brodir of Man and Sigurd himself. King Sitric was to stay in Dublin to guard the city and its people, in case the Irish sent some of their army to attack there. It was very late before the council finished and Skari had almost fallen asleep in his corner. As he dozed, pictures of Weland's house and Arna sitting by the fire drifted through his head. What a strange girl she was, and how sad she looked most of the time. It would be nice to see her smile again. He jumped as he felt his father shaking him awake.

'Go now, rest that wound while you can. We will do nothing before Friday, for the Irish are superstitious and Brian is known to be a religious man. It may be that fighting on Good Friday will make them uneasy.'

'And the battle plan will work, won't it?' said Skari.

His father shrugged. 'We're all good fighters and disciplined men. But I have yet to see a battle that did not end in chaos and mayhem. You're still limping quite a bit, aren't you? I know that wound is hurting you more than you will admit. Go to One-Eye, he'll give you some lotions for it, and something to help you sleep.'

One-Eye did give Skari both lotions and potions, and perhaps it was the potions that caused him to have such strange nightmares that night. His first dreams were sweet ones, dreams of Birsay, walking the cliffs with the wind from the sea in his face, watching for his father's ship coming in to the harbour. But then the gulls in his dreams starting shrieking, and there was blood falling from an iron-grey sky, and he could hear women screaming. He woke and found that he could not sleep again. He lay watching the clouds pass over the moon. Some of them looked like women on white horses, some like cats and some like swans, riding high in the sky. Omens for the battle? If so, what did they mean?

He thought about the Irish boy. How was he linked with him? What if he should meet him again? Would he try to kill him? He didn't want to kill him. In some other world, he thought, perhaps they could even have been friends. But not in this one. That was the way of wyrd, the fate all the Norse believed in. What was to be was to be, and there was nothing one could do about it. The best one could do was to meet one's fate with courage and dignity. The Irish boy was an enemy, a threat to Skari's brothers-in-arms. His duty was to kill him, if he met him in battle, as the boy's duty was to kill Skari. He could only hope that the battle would not bring them together. He tried to find comfort in the fact that after the battle he would be acknowledged as a full warrior. By his father, especially. That was the most important of all. Yes, there would be feasting and singing and praise, wonderful times after the battle. If he could just survive it.

CHAPTER 12

THE QUEEN'S TASK

During the next day it was much harder for Arna to get away from the house, as Birgit watched both her daughters like a hawk. She lined up so many chores to be done that Elva, who knew it was Birgit's way to keep busy when she was anxious, realised that her mother must be very anxious indeed. Arna seemed to be half asleep as she did her work, doing everything so slowly and making so many mistakes that Elva wondered if she was acting like this on purpose. Perhaps she was hoping that Birgit would give up asking her to do things. Elva could have told her that that tactic would not work with her mother. She had tried it often enough herself!

But finally Birgit ran out of things for them to do. 'Well girls, now you can do what you want until it's time to help me with the wash,' she said, 'be sure to be back for that. But don't go beyond the walls, nor near the palace. Are you listening to me now, Arna? And stay together; the streets are full of soldiers and the town is not safe. So be sure to stay together. Do you hear me now, I'm serious!'

The girls left the house together, but they were barely out the door when Arna turned to Elva and said: 'You needn't think you can stick to me like horse glue today. I have things to do that have nothing to do with you.'

Right so, said Elva to herself, let's see if I can't just follow you and see what's going on with you! Aloud she said: 'So, nothing new there, then. See if I care what you get up to!'

At least she had the satisfaction of seeing Arna's face drop in surprise.

In fact, Elva was almost sure that Arna would head straight for Queen Kormlada in the palace, so she waited just a few minutes and then started up the hill to where it stood. She caught up with Arna just in time to see her disappear into one of the side entrances, and stood, considering her next move. If she followed her, the soldiers on guard would challenge her, and she would not be allowed in. She thought back to the only time she had been in the palace. Arna and she had been sent there with some lotions of her mother's. Birgit, as well as being a healer, made beauty lotions for the skin and hair, and they were famous all over Dublin. The queen had sent for some. And never paid her mother, if Elva remembered rightly. An armed guard had brought the two of them to the queen's room. It had been large and the walls were covered in shelves, filled with all sorts of powders and potions. In the centre there was a huge loom, and the queen had been weaving something, a large banner with the symbol of a black crow against a blood-red background. Elva remembered looking out the window, down the embankment that the palace was built on. It had fascinated her, because none of the longhouses in Dublin had windows. She had been captivated by the way she could see outside, admiring the view down the bank onto a pear orchard on the other side of the ditch that surrounded the palace. The trees grew up to the level of the window. They had been heavy with fruit on that autumn day and the queen's room had been full of the scent of ripe pears. It had made her mouth water and she had badly wanted to ask for some. But they had not been offered even a drink of water, although the queen had told Arna that she was to come back to visit the following week. Elva had not been invited back again.

Now she made her way to the eastern side of the palace, where the pear orchard filled the small spit of land between the palace bank and the Salach River. The trees were in bloom, a cloud of scented whiteness against the walls of the palace. Keeping a sharp eye out for sentries, Elva scrambled up over the wall and into the orchard. She held in a shriek as she landed in some nettles, but at least she could see that it was an easy climb to where Kormlada's window looked out onto one of the taller trees. Shinning up the tree was the work of a minute, and Elva was able to settle herself very comfortably on a large branch. It swayed gently in the breeze. She looked around her: to the south the Black Pool, to the north the Liffey: and to the west the queen's chamber. The sky around her was the colour of a thrush's egg; the wind was from the south, its cold edge softened by the pale sun. A robin landed on the branch beside her, and looked at her, head to one side, as if enquiring what she was doing up here. She held her finger to her lips as if to keep him quiet and peered through the blossoms, right into the queen's room. There was a great fire burning and a huge cauldron sitting on it. Behind it she could just make out the Queen's loom. Some of the banners the Queen had woven lay around the room, marked with the symbols of Dublin: Thor's hammer, the three flames, the palace itself. Others had stranger designs – feathers and flowers and one had a white, stoat-like animal on it. Kormlada and Arna were standing together with their backs to her. The queen was braiding Arna's hair, humming gently. Elva kept as far back as she could so that if someone came into the room they would not see her among the leaves and the blossoms.

Now Arna was speaking. Elva had not heard her sound so excited in months.

'I finally got away from them all, even Elva! She's driving me mad – sometimes I get so angry with her! I'd like to nip her neck, put her out of action so that she can no longer watch me, follow me. She's always watching and waiting and I've had enough of it.'

The queen spoke, her voice low and as smooth as honey.

'It is too early to do anything like that. When you are with the Sisters, a time will come when you will have revenge on them all. You will no longer have to bear it, the closed hall and the closed minds. You will fly with the Sisters over snowy landscapes and you shall be free of all the things that have kept you trapped for so many years.'

Arna drew a deep breath. Then the two of them spoke together. It was almost a chant. Through the smell of pear blossom, Elva caught a scent of something heavy burning in the room. It made her feel sleepy.

The Sisters are weaving their web,
Their web they are weaving:
Look you: the warp is stretched
For the fall of the warriors
Wet with blood,
Our warp is bloodred,
Our weft bruise blue.
The woof is the guts
Of fair faced warriors

The warp is held down
With the skulls of the slain
We use for our spindles,
The spears of the dead men
Our reels are the arrows,
Harvested from fair flesh.
Our shuttles are swords
This warwoof we work
So weave we,
We Sisters, this battle-field banner.

They finished together and then the queen spoke: 'I swear by the Morrigan, Queen of Darkness, that you shall find your mother again, the mother your father could not change or cage.'

Arna's voice was dreamy when she answered: 'They think I don't remember her. But I do. I remember her white face and her silver eyes and her soft voice. How could they expect me to accept that fat Irish woman with her dark hair and pink cheeks as my mother? How could my father have expected that? But then he never understood me. Sometimes I think he prefers Elva to me, his own flesh and blood.'

'You must not care what your human father wishes. You will become a servant of the All-Father. And in the meantime you must do as the Sisters wish. Listen to me carefully and I will tell you what that is. You must take my cloak again, and make your way into the Irish camp. You must go and whisper defeat into the ears of the sleeping soldiers. And you must find again the Irish boy who carries the sword. This time you must succeed, Arna. I will give you no more chances. And when you have done as I wish, the Sisters will take you away. They will take you across the seas to where their hall stands in the snow. This is the hall where they bring the warriors, when they pluck their spirits from the battlefield like red flowers. In that hall, the warriors feast at night and in the morning go out and kill each other all over again. An endless cycle of the feast before the battle, the feast after the battle. And the battle, the heart of it all, always lies between. The Sisters sing for Odin the All Father, and Odin loves them; they ride with him on the wild hunt, the hounds crying and calling, across the wild skies of the North.'

'But are you sure they will take me with them? When you show them to me in the smoke, they're so bright that they blind me. Can I really go with them? It's like a dream when I see them – afterwards I don't remember what I've done. I'm afraid I'm not strong enough to be with them.'

'They will take you. You will become strong, as I have become strong, by willing yourself not to care. But first you must do what I tell you. Then you will have the strength to go to them altogether – to go onto the battlefield as a bird and eat carrion flesh so that you may become one with them. Then you will be free. Then no-one will mock your white hair, or your strange eyes.'

'Or my strange ways.' Arna's voice shook as she spoke.

'Or your strange ways.'

'I will fly with the winged ones to a place beyond, to the cold snows, to the stormy seas ...'

'But before you are free to go with them you must bring me the sword from the Irish boy, with his blood on it. And you must bring me the cloak and the ring that will come to their power on Friday, your birthday. That is the day of the battle, and I must have them then. Arna, remember, you must come to me. With these sacred things I will wake the powers that have slept for many years. I will be all-powerful. You will be free. Can I trust you to do that?'

'Yes, my queen, you can.'

'Are you sure that I can? For yesterday you did not do as the Sisters willed, did you, Arna? You did not kill the Irish boy I sent you to kill. You did not take his sword.'

Now there was a note of menace in Kormlada's voice

'I couldn't, I couldn't do it.' Arna sounded as if she was going to cry. 'I'm sorry, my queen, I couldn't. I meant to, then I couldn't help it; he was such a child. And he had smiled at me so sweetly.'

'And what about the other boy, the Norse one? Why did you not kill *him* at least and bring the prey to your Sisters, who would have petted you for such a prize?'

Arna was silent.

Kormlada's voice changed now and became colder and harsher.

'Be careful, or they will no longer be loving Sisters to you. They will beat you with their wings. Your Sisters have no time for fools and weaklings and neither do I. I need blood for the powers to be drawn to my side and I will have it! You must do better next time. Fetch them either a warrior for Valhalla or an Irish body for carrion, or by the Morrigan you will suffer for it. Next time you will feel no pity. Next time you will kill. Do you understand?'

CHAPTER 13

THE KING'S BLESSING

It was the eve of the battle. Heralds had been sent between the enemy camps. The armies would meet on the sands of Clontarf at dawn on Good Friday. The full Irish camp had now moved to the woods beside the coastline, carefully avoiding the grove that had been Tomar's Wood. Dara spent most of his time wandering around the camp – now made up of many thousands of soldiers – with his eyes wide and his mouth, as Turlough put it unkindly, open wide enough to catch a swarm of bees. But it was hard not to gaze in wonder at the gathering of these men, armies from all over Ireland and beyond the eastern seas. Dara was especially impressed by Ospak of Man, who had come over to the

Irish side, disgusted with his brother, the violent, treacherous Brodir. He was tall and fierce-looking and said very little.

Niall whispered to Dara, as they watched Ospak cleaning his sword. 'He's a great warrior, almost as dangerous as his brother! He has been giving advice to the king as to how best to attack the Norse soldiers.'

'And what advice does he give about fighting Brodir?'

'Not to do it!'

The boys laughed and Ospak looked over at them, smiling. 'Well, boys, it's good to see you laughing at such a time! It's a sign of courage, and the gods love the brave.'

'Could we have a look at your sword?' Dara asked shyly; he had noticed that it was a beautiful piece of craftsmanship.

'Come over so, it is the finest Norse work. It's my old friend Skullcleaver – it has been a good brother to me in many a battle.'

The sword was indeed beautiful, the craftsmanship superb. But when Dara handed it back to Ospak, the Manx warrior looked curiously at the sword Dara himself carried.

'That's a strange mixture of a weapon: the hilt is Norse work, but I'd lay odds the blade is Irish.'

Dara nodded, laying the sword flat so that Ospak could see it clearly. 'Yes, the hilt was my mother's – she never said where it came from, but she had it since before I was born. She had a new blade welded to it when she gave it to my brother. To Ronan.'

Dara's voice dropped at his brother's name.

'And your brother is no more?' Ospak asked.

Dara shook his head. He still couldn't speak about Ronan.

'I too have lost my brother, but to madness and magic, not death,' said Ospak sadly. 'Well, bear Ronan's sword bravely, in memory of him and the other men and boys who carried it with honour.'

All day Thursday the Irish troops patrolled the edge of the forest, where pastureland led to the beaches and the slob lands. The sky was the colour of ashes. There was a feeling of silent tension in the camp. Even the small animals and the birds seemed disinclined to move from their burrows and nests, as if nervous about what lay outside. Or ahead. There was not much left to do to prepare for the battle, which meant that there was more time to think about what was to come. The bustle of preparation had gone into a lull: the plans had been made, the soldiers informed of the tactics to be used. Dara and Niall had their own plan. It was a simple one: they just intended to rush onto the sands behind the banner of the king and attack every Norseman in sight.

'The quiet before the storm,' said Cormac, laughing. He was somebody who never showed fear. 'Though I have never seen it this calm. There's a strange feeling in the air. They say that Aoibhell, the banshee of the O'Briens, was heard crying last night. And some say a white-haired girl has been seen in the woods, surely another creature of the Good Folk. Did you hear anything strange last night, Turlough? You're an O'Brien, you should have heard the banshee, if she was at her tricks.'

Turlough shrugged, tight-lipped. Dara wondered if he had heard or seen something and didn't want to talk about it.

'These woods are strange,' Turlough said finally. 'I like them not, and I hope the battle doesn't lead us back into them.'

'Aye, I'm with you there. But the battle will be on the meadows and the sands,' said Cormac. 'We're lucky that we're fighting on the northern end; the sands are firm and yellow there; southwards, closer to Liffey, they're muddier, and they stink. It's much harder to fight when you can't get a proper foothold. You will both advance with me, for I am to lead the youngest soldiers. Dara, your father will go forward, ahead of us, with Prince Murrough. The forces of Meath are to come in from the North and fight with us. With so many men we're bound to win.'

But later that day a rumour started in the camp which made everyone's heart sink. It seemed that Malachy of Meath had changed his mind. He was not going to fight alongside King Brian. There were different versions as to what had happened. No-one seemed to know the full story. Or if they did, they were not telling anyone. Some said that there had been some kind of dispute between Malachy and Prince Murrough. Everyone knew that Murrough's tongue often ran away with him. Perhaps the row was about who would have the high kingship if Brian was killed. Brian had already sent for his other son, Donagh, who was fighting the forces of Leinster in the hills south of Dublin, to come up to join them, but the whole camp knew he would never make it to Clontarf in time for the battle. The other news, even more disheartening to Dara, was that Brian himself was too ill to fight. He would stay nearby in the wood and pray for the success of his army.

'He's an old man,' said Cormac. 'He knows he would do more harm than good going into battle. Too many people would be needed to protect him from the enemy. Murrough is a great soldier; he has the strength of an ox, and the courage too, and he'll lead us well.'

But Dara was desperately disappointed. Every time he had thought of the battle, he had imagined Brian leading them forward, riding his great white horse, the blue banners of the Dalcassians fluttering all around them in the wind from the sea. Murrough, Turlough's father, did not have the charm of either his father or his son. He was quick-tempered and had a nasty side to his tongue. And he was not able to put heart into the warriors when they no heart left, the way his father could.

Cormac saw Dara's disappointed face and said: 'Aye, it's

a pity. We must just hope that Brian's prayers are as good as his sword hand was, when he was in his prime. Come with me to his tent, Dara, we must get you his blessing before the battle. Tomorrow there will be no time.'

When they got to the royal tent, the king looked old and tired, and his old servant, Laidean, was fussing over him.

'Let them come in,' said Brian when the old man tried to prevent Cormac and Dara from entering the tent. 'Let them have my blessing, for there is very little I can do for them now but pray for them. It is a sad day when the king cannot fight with his people. But here I will pray, in this heathen place, that my people will have victory and that the Norse kings will leave our lands, and leave us to live peaceful lives. I will pray that this will indeed be the battle to end battles. Here, child, come and I will bless you.'

The high king put his hands on Dara's head and closed his eyes, whispering the holy words. But halfway through he stopped, and held Dara from him, looking at him intently. 'There is some other kind of magic at work here. And you are part of it. Part of the old magic that came to me last night. It was the banshee, Aoibhell, the woman who guards my people, who came and talked to me.'

'What did she say to you?' Dara's voice was barely a whisper. He could not believe that the great King Brian was confiding in him.

'That I cannot tell you.'

The king looks so sad and tired, thought Dara. Greatly daring, he took Brian's hand and kissed it. The old king smiled.

'Sit with me a while, child.' So Dara sat and the king looked into the glowing embers of the fire that had been lit to keep the chill out of his bones. He began to talk then, half to himself: 'What is this war about? A missing button, a lost game of chess? A whiplash? A rash word said? A guest gone without bidding a courteous farewell? Four small things to lead to so many dead. But perhaps when this is done I will have peace at last. There must be peace and there must be forgiveness.'

The king fell silent, and Dara dared to ask: 'Do you forgive Mael Mordha, King Brian?'

'Mael Mordha? I forgave him long ago. But I must go on with the battle, or my people will be put at risk. And my tributes will be taken from me. I am Brian of the Tributes: I would lose my name. What is a king without tributes and power? We are all caught now, caught in a web that we cannot escape. But child, remember this: battle is ugly, but you will see beauty there: the courage of men, their loyalty to each other. Self sacrifice, even to death. And nobleness of spirit: for to believe in something is good, and to stand by your king is the code we all live by. I know all this. I have lived by this, the code of the warrior and the leader of my people. But I am weary of battles, always battles. I would that my crown could pass peacefully to Murrough, and that he would wear it in peace. But I see a cruel death for him, for his words are rash and his temper is short.'

Again there was silence, and Dara asked: 'And Turlough? What do you see for him?'

Brian's face lit up. 'Ah, he is a fine boy, and he will be a fine man. For him I see much honour and glory, and a great kingdom, if his own courage does not lead him into rashness. If he were only a little older, he and not his father should be my heir. But I should not be laying all this worry and grief on you, boy. Tomorrow will be a great day for you.'

He stood up, and called to Cormac: 'Do this for me. Tell them to keep the young boys at the back of the ranks. Christ, to see the flower of youth mown down on such a lovely strand, and on such a holy day. Perhaps we will all suffer tomorrow to rise to joy again on Sunday. Perhaps, perhaps it will be so. I pray it will be so.'

Cormac and Dara bowed low.

And Dara said: 'You are my king and I am happy to serve you with my life's blood if that is what is needed.'

'Let us hope, child, that it is not.'

CHAPTER 14

THE RIDER ON THE SHORE

If the men in the Irish camps were anxious and unsettled, there was trouble in the Norse camp too.

In fact, thought Skari, the camp is in a state of near chaos, and it is mostly because of that idiot, Brodir. Brodir, whose eyes were so strange: blank dark pools or wild, glinting red, Brodir, whose long black hair flew across his face as he rampaged through the camp, ready to fight anyone who got in his way. These last nights he had stayed up in a trance, seeing things the others could not, sometimes screaming and writhing in agony, shouting so loudly that the whole camp woke up. And his men were no better. All through Tuesday and Wednesday night they had shrieked in their sleep, and when they were woken by their companions they had talked of strange visions. All of them had dreamt the same dream. Scalding blood was raining down on their heads and though they had raised their shields to protect themselves, it poured down their faces. One of the men had flung himself into the sea to escape the torment, and he had not been seen since. On Wednesday night it had been even worse. That night the Manxmen dreamt that their weapons were attacking them, that their own swords leapt from their sheaths, and their axes and spears flew about in the air and tried to kill them. In the morning they had jumped at the slightest noise and spent their time picking fights with everyone.

And then they had started picking on One-Eye.

'Hey, old man,' Brodir taunted, pricking him with his sword. 'Hey, have you read the runes then? Seen the victory? Surprised you can see anything, with that rheumy eye of yours!' He laughed and hit the old man hard with his blade.

Skari, though he had no love for One-Eye, came forward with his sword drawn.

'Leave him alone,' he said, his voice more shaky than he would have liked it to be. 'He's not doing you any harm!'

Brodir turned on him: 'So it's dogboy, who doesn't recognise a great queen when he sees one! Are you One-Eye's son then, that you rush to his defence?'

The other warriors clustered around, and Skari felt his heart thumping in his chest like a drum. He tried to speak but no sound came out of his throat.

'Enough of that, Brodir. Leave the old man and the boy alone. Save your anger for the enemy; you will have a use for your rage soon enough.'

The voice was that of the Jarl of the Orkneys, Sigurd the Stout. Sigurd had been making his way through the ranks, trying to calm those who had lost their nerve.

'Come.' He turned to Brodir's men. 'You should not fear. You fight with me under the safety of the raven banner, made by my mother, who was strong in magic.'

One-Eye whispered to Skari, 'It's true, they say his mother was an Irish witch, and she made a banner for him that would bring him victory. But it is also said that whoever carries it for the jarl is bound to die himself. But wouldn't that be a sacrifice worth making!'

'Who will carry it tomorrow?'

'His herald.'

'Does he know the spell attached to it?'

One-Eye nodded. 'Yes, he is ready to die for the jarl. That is what battle is about.'

Skari nodded. That was what he had always been taught: loyalty to his lord and his fellow-warriors. But did that mean he had to defend Brodir to the death? The encounter with the Manx warrior had left Skari feeling sick and shaken, and by evening he thought his head was going to explode with the tension and anger that seemed to fill the air of the camp.

Everywhere he went there was someone chanting or drinking or sacrificing to the gods. He knew he had to get away. So he walked across to the side of the island facing land. It was only a short distance across to the shore and Skari was used to icy water. Swimming always cleared his head and a walk along the sands would surely help to do the same. He dived into the freezing water and covered the distance in minutes. Reaching the shore, he made his way northwards along the long grey beach that edged the pasture and woodland, crunching shells and seaweed under his feet, breathing in the fresh salt air and listening to the lonely cries of the gulls. He knew he should not be walking this way on his own, but he could not have borne being stuck on the ship or the island for another minute.

But now, as he walked on the beach, he wondered how much honour and glory there would be in the battle tomorrow. Since the encounter in the woods, he knew more about fighting, real fighting, not sword practice or imaginary battles. For a moment, trapped under the Irish boy with a knife digging into his flesh, he had looked his own death in the face. It had not been a pleasant feeling.

Glancing westwards, he realised that the sun was starting to go down. It was time to turn and go back to the camp. The light from the dying sun lit the city from behind, making it look like something from a dream or a vision. He kicked at the shells and stones that littered the beach as he walked along with his head down. Suddenly, he realised that there was a tall, cloaked figure coming towards him along the sands. The man was holding the bridle of a most beautiful grey horse, which walked at the same pace as the man, tossing his head occasionally, sniffing the wind. Skari could not see the man's face, for it was hidden under a grey hood. He found his hand was grasping his knife. Was this an Irishman? The figure continued to come closer. He tried to judge the strength of the stranger: tall, yes, but thin and handicapped by the hand on the horse. Should he just move away, towards the woods? No, he could not do that. That would be cowardice.

Now man and boy were almost face to face. A voice came from under the hood.

'Do not fear me, child. I mean you no harm. But I have come to give you some advice, for tomorrow will be a cruel day for you.'

No matter how he tried, Skari could not see beneath the hood. Yet, now the man had spoken, he felt his fear melt away.

'What is it you wish to tell me?' he asked.

'You must ask your father for the sword your mother left you.'

'What sword?'

'The sword that was broken and must be mended once more. The sword that was stolen and taken from the place where it should lie. I can tell you no more, but if your friends play their part, you will know everything tomorrow. There is a queen who wants to wake what should be left to sleep in peace. If she succeeds there will be doom and pain and endless war. If she has her way, tomorrow's battle will not bring peace but will be the beginning of great horror. Now, go back to the camp, and go safely, child.'

'May I not see you face?' asked Skari.

'Aye, a little, perhaps.' The figure pulled his hood slightly back.

Skari had a sense of infinite pain and wisdom, of age and of grief. And of only one bright eye, as grey as iron, looking out from under the coarse grey hood. And then, quick as a flash of lightning, the figure leapt onto his horse, as swiftly as a young boy. With a loud neigh the horse galloped into the sea ... and then … then … was somehow not there anymore. There was the blue line of sky and sea, darkening now into sunset, and the red fire behind the trees of Tomar's Wood, and the seagulls calling with their lonely cries, like women wailing for their lost loved ones. But of the grey horseman there was no sign. Skari, his head bent in thought, continued slowly on his way back towards the ships.

CHAPTER 15

IN THE HOUSE OF THE WISE WOMAN

Elva was furious with her sister. She could still hear Arna's voice in her head, repeating the horrible things she had said about her in Kormlada's room. Arna must hate her, she thought, she must really hate her. Where was the big sister she thought she once knew? The one who was brave and clever and funny? She felt as if Arna's words had torn a layer of skin from her body, so that every part of her ached with pain and anger. And hatred of Arna. Or was it hatred? Because even though she was so angry, she knew she could not leave her sister caught in Kormlada's dark web. She did not understand all the talk of the Sisters and battle, but it seemed that Arna might be lost forever if something was not done, and done quickly. Should she speak to her mother or father? Surely there was something they could do? Could they stop Arna getting away? They had not managed to stop her yet. Elva sighed. What could she do? She decided to go to the wash house, hoping to find Arna there. Maybe if she talked to her she could make her see some sense. How strange it was for her mother to be washing clothes when thousands of soldiers were preparing to fight in a great battle outside the walls of the city. Who knew what the next day might bring? She shivered, wondering about the Orkney boy, Skari. He must be getting ready for battle now. And the other boy, the Irish one, the one she had met in the forest by moonlight. Either the Irish or the Norse would win, which meant that one or other of the boys would either die or begin a life of slavery. She shivered again.

But when she reached the wash house there was no sign of Arna. Before her mother could spot her and rope her in for more chores, Elva slipped away. There was only one thing to do now, though it was not an appealing prospect. The only person who could help her now was Magrit, the Volva, the Wise Woman of Dublin.

She filched some fresh honey cakes, left cooling on the table, and fled away from the house, followed by the protesting shrieks of Astrid, who had spotted her theft. Volvas lived on the offerings of those who came to ask them for advice, and everyone knew Birgit's hammer cakes were the best in

Dublin. The Volva's grubby shack was built right against the wall of the city, as if the house itself wasn't sure it wanted to be part of the town. Elva couldn't blame it for that. It was situated in one of the nastier parts of Dublin; the fish market was on one side, a tannery on the other. The view from the front door was of the crumbling wall of a pigsty. The smells of all these places competed with each other to be the strongest and most disgusting. Elva had only been inside the Volva's house once or twice, delivering gifts from her mother. Neither Birgit nor Weland exactly approved of Magrit, though they did give her food and medicines. Her house was tiny and dark and smelled of a mixture of cat and the herbs Magrit burned to bring on her trances. In the trances she claimed she could see what was happening far away and even into the future.

Three ravens, perched on the roof of the house, cawed loudly as Elva knocked cautiously on the door of the hut. It opened immediately, and Magrit was standing there, her grey hair hanging in two thin braids on either side of her lined, dirty-brown face.

'Ah, little Elva. I was expecting you,' she said to Elva. 'Come in, come in.' Elva silently handed her the cakes. 'Thanks to you, child, that is kind of you. Fierce kind to a poor old woman.'

She stood smiling her gap-toothed smile, her shoulders stooped as if carrying the weight of the world.

Elva hated the way she bowed and scraped to everyone, flattering her visitors shamelessly in the hope of getting more gifts out of them. When she had come here once with Arna, Magrit had held her sister's face to the light and sworn that she could see her fate, a marriage to a prince of royal blood. She had gone on and on about her sister's pretty face and winning ways. Yet she had sneaked on Arna: she was the one who had told their mother that Arna had gone to see Kormlada. Now she poured a cup of water for Elva. Elva could not help noticing the cup was filthy, but politeness made her pretend to drink it.

Magrit said: 'Now, my dear one, what is it you wish for?' She pushed her cat, as old and scraggy as herself, off the wooden bench in order to leave it free for Elva. 'Here, Grimalkin, move out of the way, let the little lady be seated. How are all you family? Your father, your mother, your beautiful sister?'

'They are all well, thank you,' said Elva, and then suddenly burst out, 'Well, they're not really. It's Arna ... she has become ... very ... strange. She keeps disappearing at night. I have seen her in the Irish camp, whispering into the ears of the soldiers, blowing on their faces. She seems to be able to change into a sort of white animal. I think Queen Kormlada has given her something that makes her able to do that.'

'Ah, the queen. Always at the centre of whatever mischief is brewing. And Arna is a girl likely to be used by such a one. It's coming up to her thirteenth birthday, isn't it? 'Twas bound to happen, the fates wove her future long before now. But let us look in the bowl and see what we may see.'

She took the silver bowl she used for the scrying and filled it with water. But just as she took a bundle of herbs from the ceiling and was about to set them alight from the fire, there was a sharp rat-tat-tat. She dropped the herbs and stood stock-still, as if frozen.

'What is it, Magrit? What has frightened you?' Elva could see that the Volva was pale beneath the grime.

The rapping starting again, louder this time, more impatient. But the noise was not coming from the front door, but from a tall cupboard in the wall.

Magrit stood, then gathered Grimalkin tight, as if she was trying to gather courage into her heart.

She went to the door of the cupboard and opened it. Elva, peering through the darkness, could see now that it was not a cupboard at all. Behind the door there was another door, and that was where the tapping noise was coming from.

'Tell nobody of this,' said Magrit, her voice hardly more than a whisper. She pulled open the second door.

Standing there was a man in a grey cloak. His hood was pulled down over his head and he leaned on a staff. There was a white raven perched on his shoulder.

Magrit was even paler now. She bowed low.

'My Lord ...' The words came out half-strangled in her

throat. The hooded man bowed his head slightly, acknowledging the greeting.

'Magrit. Still brewing potions and burning weeds.' He sighed. 'You might ask me to come in.'

'Of course, my Lord. Enter ... This is–' She was interrupted.

'I know very well who she is, Magrit. Hello, Elva, I have been watching you and your sister for some time. You wish to save her from Kormlada, do you not?'

Elva could still not see the man's face. But his voice was kind. And Magrit seemed in awe of him. Perhaps he could help her save her sister.

'Yes, I do. Can you tell me what's happening with her? And what I can do?'

'I can tell you what you can try to do. There are no guarantees that it will work. There are forces taking your sister away from you, away from ordinary life. They are very strong and guard her well. And she herself does not want to be saved from them. She wants to go with the women who wear the swan cloaks. But she does not realise that she is not truly one of them. Kormlada has lied to her, and has made her many false promises. She has made your sister deny her human blood. Arna is in danger of leaving you altogether to become something else, something that Kormlada will control. Control is what Kormlada wants, power over every living thing. She wishes to do evil, to raise things that should be left to sleep. She is a queen without a kingdom, and her love of power will not tolerate that. Arna's collar and a certain sword will help her to win one – but she also needs blood, and I fear she will either send Arna to fetch that for her, or use Arna's own.'

'But who are the swan girls? And why does Arna want so badly to be one of them? She was talking about them in the palace, and I hadn't a clue really about what she was on about ...'

There was a smile in the man's voice. 'Ah, people are losing the knowledge of their stories. My time in Dublin has indeed come to an end. Did you never hear of the Valkyries, the maidens who ride in the wild hunt with Odin, and carry the bodies of the slain from battle? They are the Sisters of Storm. They bring the warriors to Valhalla, where they fight and feast forever. They are cruel and fierce and know no human love, and your sister has given her heart to them. Her body will follow soon; but her human blood is too warm for her to become truly one of them. She will be left outside the hall of the gods, a lost spirit, howling in the darkness. Kormlada has tricked her: she is using her to find something that will give her the power to win the battle tomorrow. When she finds it she will have no more use for Arna.'

'So what can I do? I don't want her to die!'

The old man's voice was suddenly very serious. 'Would

you not be happy to be the only girl, the only daughter in the house of your father and mother? Would it not be easier for you not to have Arna around? And do you not feel angry with her for her treatment of you?'

Elva shook her head vehemently. 'It might be easier but it's not what I want. Of course I'm angry with her but I love Arna. Even if she has become so mean this last while, even if I feel I hate her sometimes. She wasn't always like that. And my mother says that sometimes it's not what you feel but what you do that's important. We can't help what we feel, but we can choose how we act. So I choose to try to help her. And anyway, she's my sister!'

'She has no blood tie to you!'

'She's still my sister. The only one I have. We grew up together. And all I know is that I must try to save her. You must tell me how I can help her – stop these swan maidens from taking her away. And what exactly is Kormlada going to do? What does she want?'

'She wants to raise the afterwalkers who dwell in Tomar's Grove, those spirits that should be left to rest quietly, now their time in the world is done. If she raises that army of ghosts, she will win the battle and take control of all Ireland. She and Brodir will rule this gentle land, and everyone, Norse and Irish, will become a slave to their cruelty and their lust for power.'

'But that mustn't happen!'

'No, it must not. But you cannot stop it unless you can stop Arna bringing the sword and ring to Kormlada. And that will be no easy task. You must go to the Grove tomorrow and stop them both. Now, I must leave you. I have many tasks to finish tonight.'

And then he was gone. Elva did not see him opening the door. Magrit was looking as pale as death, clutching her filthy cat to her heart, and shaking with fear.

'Who was that? How do you know him? How does he know so much about Arna and me?' Elva fired the questions at Magrit.

'He has many names. The All-Seeing One is one, though he has but one eye. I never thought to see him come here, to my door.'

'But what did he mean me to do for Arna? How can I stop her? How can I stop the queen?'

Magrit shrugged. 'That is something you must find out for yourself, for I do not know. Now, begone.' She poured herself something from one of the jugs on the table and drank it quickly. Her voice sharpened: 'I said begone, child! My nerves will not be the better of that meeting for many days!'

Elva left the Volva's house with her head bent and her mind in a whirl. She had not understood everything the cloaked man had told her, but she had understood enough to realise that Arna's body and spirit were both in deadly danger. She decided she had to tell her parents what was happening. She could not do this alone.

But when she got home she found the house in panic: Weland was very ill. He lay on his bed, gasping for breath, with Birgit, pale and for once silent, trying every medicine she knew in a vain attempt to ease his pain and get air into his lungs. Though he was covered in furs, he was also deathly cold, shaking so much that the furs kept falling off the bed.

'This fever has been coming on him for days,' said Birgit. 'But of course he refused to say anything about it. Lord knows what he has caught: I have never seen anything like it in all my years.'

When Elva went over to him, he caught her arm, and whispered through his gasps for breath: 'Find Arna for me, Elva, find Arna.'

Elva nodded. While her mother was busy with her father she went to the chest. The lock was broken, and the necklace, the white feather cloak and the catskin gloves, everything was gone. So Arna had them and had left to go to Kormlada already. But lying in the bottom, something glinted like fire. She reached down into the darkness. Yes, there was definitely something there. Something she hadn't seen before – a ring, a small golden ring. She picked it up: it looked just the right size to fit her middle finger. But this was not a closed ring – it had a small open section, as if it was meant to attach to something else. She looked at it where it lay in her palm. At first she thought that the gold was unmarked, but now she could see runes written on it. Or were they tiny figures of birds, dancing around its inside, hidden when it was worn? She slipped it onto her finger, and the metal, cool at first, warmed quickly. Now it seemed to glow even more brightly. It somehow gave her courage. She knew what she had to do.

But when she reached her tunnel under the walls, there were sentries blocking the way. They told her that it was too late for a young girl like her to be out.

'Don't you know there's to be a battle tomorrow, child? Get safe home as fast as you can!'

She left them but she did not go home. Instead she went back to Magrit's house. When she knocked, there was no answer, so, curled in her cloak, she waited by the pigsty wall opposite, trying hard to ignore the smell and the noise the pig family made. Sitting there reminded her of the times she had been locked outside the warmth of the houses, begging in the street with her mother. But now she was locked inside the walls. And that was not a good feeling either. Now she knew how Arna felt, blocked, locked in, unable to move freely. The sun went down and she fell into an uneasy sleep.

Your ring is glowing, Elva.

It was Arna's voice.

It was so wonderful, Elva. I stood with them, my Sisters, and they held out their feathered arms to me and stood in a circle around me while Kormlada clasped the collar around my throat. As it closed, the singing began, the voices of the swan maidens, the most beautiful music! Music that can only be heard by humans when they are taken away to the fields of Odin. It was so lovely and so lonely that tears came to my eyes, and Kormlada said: 'Do not cry, for tears are for humans.' And then they put the cloak over my shoulders, and I felt myself rising with them, felt my feet leave the ground as I moved my wings and found myself rising, above the trees of the pear grove. How small and far away it all was, so soon: the wood, the sea, the town of Dublin. A toy a child might play with, and tumble over, and all the people, with all their little lives, so very far beneath me! There was the curve of the bay and the shining sea; there was the hill of Howth ... and the river was no more than a silver trail of tears or water spilt from a cup, flowing into the sea. All so small: none of it mattered. I flew higher and higher and my Sisters flew with me, and I never wanted it to end, for I felt freer than I had ever felt. So free!

Elva woke with a start: the sun was rising, and Magrit was standing looking down at her. She did not look at all pleased to see Elva again. That's her real face, thought Elva. Not the false smile, not the simpering voice, but a hard, cold eye and an abrupt: 'What do you want now?'

'You have to let me out the door that opens to the woods,' she told her. 'If you do not I will tell everyone about it and the king will make you close it up.'

The Volva looked at her, and then shrugged.

'You do this at your peril, you know that, don't you? The chances of saving your sister are small, and you risk your own life by leaving the safety of the city.'

'I know,' said Elva. 'But I have to try.'

PART FOUR
23 APRIL 1014

FRJADAGR
DÉ hAOINE
FRIDAY

CHAPTER 16

CALL TO ARMS

In the camp of Brodir's men, it had been yet another terrible night, the most terrible yet. In the middle of the night, the warriors leapt up, screaming that battle ravens had come to attack them with beaks and claws made of iron. Another man jumped into the water to escape the demons, and drowned. Brodir swore that the gods would accept his death as a sacrifice and it augured well for the battle. But others said it was a sign that they would fight and die, and that bird-demons would drag them all to hell.

One-Eye had wept and rocked through the night, foretelling doom until the waning moon gave way to a red sunrise over the bay of Dublin. Skari looked to the east and the north, and listened to his companions as they prayed to Odin for victory. Sigurd himself was sacrificing to Odin, the wise man watching him with one red eye.

'Earl Sigurd, your own mother was an Irish Volva, and she foretold your doom. She wove your fate into the very fabric of the raven banner your herald carries before you in battle. Beware that it does not come upon you in this meeting.'

'Old one, no man knows when his doom is to come,' said Sigurd. 'But we must meet it with courage. If it comes to me while I am in battle I know that the Valkyries will bring me to feast with Odin in Valhalla.'

'Brave words,' said the old man. 'We shall see if you live up to them.'

Then, when Sigurd left, he began again, muttering and chanting. Skari could not help but hear him, though he wanted to stop his ears.

'I see a man in Caithness,' One-Eye whispered, 'who saw the jarl and his soldiers, riding a fine white horse he was, and he followed him under the hill ... He will not be seen again, for he has followed Sigurd into the darkness ... And at Swinefell the priests' cloaks are covered in blood ... And in the Southern Isles, Jarl Gilli has had a terrible dream. A man came to him; a man called Hostfinn, and said he had seen white-haired maidens singing a war song.'

One-Eye paused, then shook himself, like a dog shaking off a dream. When he spoke again, his voice was softer: 'Aye, look, the queen is coming, to bring wine to the jarl and give him courage in battle. I saw her last evening on the sands.

She met a cloaked man, riding a grey horse.'

'Who was the man?' asked Skari, wondering if it had been the man he himself had met.

'Who knows? There are those that say it was Malachy, that she has made a treaty with him! Her daughter is married to him now, as she was once.' One-Eye snorted. 'Whoever he was, we can be sure the queen was up to no good ...'

Kormlada came on board Sigurd's ship, dressed in jewels and fine silks. She looked younger than the last time he had seen her, thought Skari; her cheeks were plumper, her hair the glossy black of a raven's wing.

It's as if she feeds on battles, thought Skari. It's all very well for her; she's not going to risk her life. She just sends others out to be killed.

When she left, Skari noticed she went towards Tomar's Wood, not towards the town. He stood staring after her, at the fields and sands where they would meet the Irish.

His father came up behind him and clamped his hand on Skari's shoulder: 'Well, boy, are you ready? No sick stomach or dizziness? Clear head and steady hand?'

Skari nodded. He would rather die than admit to his father that his stomach had been in a knot for days now.

Ragnall laughed. 'It suits you well to pretend you're not frightened, but remember fear can be an ally too in battle. Yes, we must lose ourselves in the fight. Yes, we must let the spirit of the Valkyries take us over. But there may come a time when the wisest and the best thing to do is to flee, if all is lost. Skari, be brave but not too brave. Be brave but not foolish.'

'If it is my fate that we do not meet after this fight,' he continued, 'I want you to go home to Birsay, to be the master of our lands in my place. You must care for the flocks and finish the spring ploughing. You will be a young lord, but I know you will be a just and good one.'

Skari felt tears prick his eyes, and concentrated hard on making sure they did not fall. It was only after his father left that he remembered he had forgotten to ask him about his mother's sword. But there was no time to follow him. The sun had fully risen and the tide was coming out and it was time to leave the ship and wade through the shallow water in towards the Meadow of the Bull. The Irish tribes were already moving out from the woods, down through the meadows and onto the shore of the sea.

Now it was time to make ready, to make sure his sword could not be sharper nor his spirit more prepared. Usually Hermund was there to do the final check with him. Now there was no-one. Skari felt very alone. He pulled his leather helmet on and made a last check of his shield, his sword and his dagger. Then he made his way forward, keeping pace with the line-up of soldiers he had been allotted to fight with. His father had moved closer to where Lord Sigurd's raven banner flew high in the wind. Ragnall's own herald was there, carrying the family banner, a seahorse swimming against dark blue waves. A flock of white birds flew overhead; so swiftly that Skari could not make out what they were, though he thought they were too large for seagulls. They called out in unison and their cry shook him to the core. It was so lonely, so lost. As if they were already mourning the dead.

Now the heralds began the roll-call of those who were going into battle:

… Amlaff, son of Sitric Silkbeard;

Mael Mordha King of Leinster;

Jarl Sigurd the Stout of Orkney;

Brodir of Man;

Dolait, Asgal, sons of Gofraidh, Lord of the Land of Snow;

The Lords of the Isles of Cats, Lewis, Kintyre and Argyll;

Carol and Anwud, son of Eabhac of Norway;

Thorstein, son of Hall of the Side in Iceland …

CHAPTER 17

THE MEADOW OF THE BULL

… Conaing and Turlough, Princes of the Dalcassians;

Murrough, Prince and heir to Brian;

The sons of the King Brian – Donal, Conor, Tadhg and Flann;

Conaing, the son of Donn Cuan;

Ospak of Man …

The Irish heralds were also calling the names of those who would go into battle, a seemingly endless list of chieftains, of Dalcassian princes, of warriors from all over Ireland. But Malachy's men were not on the list. The massed ranks were still encamped on the flat fields of Fingal, to the north of Tomar's Wood; and at their head Malachy stood and watched, but gave no order to join the ranks of the high king.

Like Skari, Dara was listening to the names and watching the sun rise. The high king rode through the ranks of the army on his great white horse, his sword in one hand and a cross in the other, giving his blessing to them all. Beside him rode his herald, carrying the blue banner. It would be carried into the battle by Murrough's herald. Just looking at the king made Dara feel more solid, as if the earth beneath his feet were steadier. Yes, there is fear, thought Dara, fear and yet excitement. No-one knew what would happen on this day. No-one knew who would still be alive when night fell. But now, at least, everything was simple. There was only one thing left to do: to fight as best one could. Thinking of what had been or what might be had no place here.

The armies stood massed on either side of the broad meadows that led down to the beaches and the mudflats, the Meadow of the Bull. Ireland had never seen a battle like it. Thousands of men and boys, armed and ready. And all still, all waiting for the battle to begin. They stood and watched each other for what felt like a very long time. The banners on either side blew briskly in the wind: blue and blood-red and bright green and gold. Dara could see the raven on the

Jarl of Orkney's banner and wondered if the Orkney boy was there. If he met him in battle, what would he do? For Dara had been thinking hard about the boy and about Cormac's reaction to him. He had remembered how his mother had been a slave in the northern isles before she came home and married his father. And how sometimes she cried out in the night, calling for her lost son. She had done that even before his brother Ronan was killed. Now Dara felt almost sure the child she called out for was Skari.

And if Skari was his half-brother, and he met him in battle, would he kill him?

Dara's division was furthest north, directly opposite the Orkney one. To the south of the jarl's men were Brodir and his wild Manxmen. Next to Dara's division was the main Munster contingent, led by Murrough, and to the south of that the ranks of the princes of Connacht. The Norse mercenaries were the last battalion, the one closest to the city. They were lined up opposite those Dublin soldiers who had come to do battle, led by Sitric's son. Between the Dubliners and the Orkney warriors were the Leinstermen, led by Mael Mordha. Dara was proud to be fighting with Turlough and the other members of Brian's closest family, though, as Brian had commanded, he was being kept to the back with the other younger boys. Niall stood beside him, talking nineteen to the dozen, shaking with excitement.

'This way, if we need to run, we will be first to get away!'

he had joked. But Dara knew that neither he nor Niall would run away, no matter how desperate the situation might become. He would keep fighting until he fell, or the Irish were triumphant. And of course they would win. Wouldn't they? He made a picture in his head to give himself courage: Brian's face, smiling when they brought the news of the victory to him.

And then there was a moment when it felt as if the very air was frozen, as if even the banners did not move, as if the sea held its breath and the sun stopped in its course. A Norseman shouted an insult across the meadow, and the Irish shouted a battle cry back, and the two armies advanced towards each other, while the white gulls swirled over the shore and the bright sea.

The first soldiers met in a kind of stately dance. One-to-one, the warriors faced each other in single combat – a battle fought arm to arm, man to man. But soon, what had started as a stately dance became something else. The two armies rushed at each other, howling their battle-cries above the crashing of the waves and the cries of the gulls.

Dara's eyes were blinded with dazzling light as he marched forward; it was the sun, reflecting on shields and armour, directly in their faces as they faced the Norse. Swords were flashing against each other in the bright light, as if they were setting off sparks. Jarl Sigurd's raven flapped its wings in the wind that suddenly rose, biting its way down from the north and the east, bringing black clouds. And on the winds flocks of dark birds flew over the warriors, filling the air with their shrieks, scenting the blood and watching for those who were already starting to fall, like tall trees cut down by the axes of the enemy.

As the clouds moved across the sun, Dara, still held to the rear of the battle by Turlough's command, could see clearly how the Norse fought. They sent the heavily armoured and armed soldiers in first, forming what they called shieldburgs around their leaders. The men stood close together, ringing their lord, their shields locked together. Unlike the Irish, only some of whom wore armour, they mostly wore chain-mail and helmets. Javelins flew through the air with a vicious whistling, but the main sound was battleaxe against shield, sword against shield, spears against shield. Grunts of effort and furious battle-cries, sometimes changing to screams as metal pierced flesh. Dara tried to keep the picture of Brian in his head, his sword in one hand, his crucifix in the other. God would keep them safe surely, and give them the victory. Then Turlough raised his arm and waved his sword, and their battalion moved forward, into the heart of the fight.

Now the warriors were packed in together, sword to sword, shield to shield. The only thought that there was room for was of survival. The fighters lashed out with their swords, all the tricks of the weapon masters forgotten in the need to keep sharp blades from soft flesh. The blood rage grew in Skari: he felt wings swooping over his head and thought of the Valkyries, the shield maidens, flying above him, urging him on. He spotted the prince who had captured him in the forest – the son of Brian's son. A good prize. Yet as he moved forward, Turlough disappeared behind the bulk of a red-haired Munsterman, three times as big as Skari. As he lunged at Skari, Skari managed to flick his sword out of his hand and began to pursue him as he ran from the field. But then he stopped in his tracks. Throughout the battle, he had kept watching for the banner of their house: a white seahorse on a background of blue waves. As long as it was upright Skari knew that his father was still fighting, for his herald never left his side. But now he realised that he could not see it any more. As his eyes scanned the wasteland of battling warriors and fallen bodies, Skari saw it had fallen. It was lying on the sands, still feebly fluttering in the wind.

Skari ran to where it lay: Farhal the herald was there, his throat slit open, and beside him lay his father, a great gash in his leg and another in his arm. Worst of all, his helmet was gone and his head was covered in blood. His eyes were open, and as Skari knelt beside him his father grasped his hand and with agonising slowness lifted his other hand. His bloody fingers marked his blessing on Skari's forehead.

'Son, there is something I have to tell you. It's about the Irish boy.'

'Don't talk, Father, save your strength. I must try to get you to the ships.'

Skari looked up despairingly towards where the ships bobbed on the water of the bay. Even as he said the words, he knew it was hopeless.

His father managed a smile. 'No, sit still for a moment. Listen. It will be the last time I ask something of you, my brave son.' Ragnall stopped, gulped, catching air into his lungs. 'It's a tale from the past. From your past. Your mother is not dead, Skari. She was taken back to Ireland. I took her on a raid with me. It was when you were just a baby. She didn't want to leave you, but I … I made her. I wanted her with me. I was always afraid. Afraid she would leave me. 'Twould have been better to leave her in Orkney.'

He paused, gasping for air, and Skari said: 'Father, let me get you some water … don't try to talk …'

'Water no use. We were attacked. When the fighting was over, your mother was … gone. I don't know what happened. Whether she was captured or went willingly. She never came back.'

There was a pause. Skari suddenly realised he knew what his father was going to say.

'The boy Dara is her child. She must have married this Cathal and had more children. That boy is your half-brother,

Skari. That is why the Irish would not kill you – you have their blood in you.'

'But that can't be possible!'

His father managed a smile, then grimaced as a wave of pain came over him. 'Your mother was from Dalcassia. She would have made her way back there. She had one blue and one green eye. She left something behind. A sword blade, a blade without a hilt. I had a new hilt made for it and it is the sword I carry. You must take it now. Fight bravely with it.'

These last words were no more than a whisper; Skari could see that his father's strength had almost gone.

Skari knelt beside him. There was nothing to be done but hold his father in his arms until it was over. But just before he lost consciousness, his father whispered fiercely: 'Go, boy, go now and defend yourself. Bring back my love to Ingrid and to little Gudrun. Go home to Lambsfell; look after the flocks and the crops. Go home.'

And Skari covered his father's face with his cloak, took the sword from his side, and went again into the battle.

And the battle continued, hour after hour, while the sun rose high in the sky and then began its slow journey westwards, behind Dublin and the forest.

Dara drew a breath and looked around him. So this is a

battle, a real battle: not the brave banners flying, not the high ideals and noble words, not the singing, not the victory feast. This was the smell of death, men lying opened like meat on a butcher's slab. He had already seen terrible pictures, pictures that would stay in his mind forever. Pictures of horror, of death and pain and despair. But as Brian had said, he had also seen pictures of courage and loyalty. Ferdia holding his comrade Finn in his arms, shaking him, telling him to wake up. As a Norse soldier came up towards Fergus's back, ready to stab him between the shoulder blades, Finn's brother cut him off, and for his trouble felt that same sword piercing his own heart. There were brave deeds and deeds of absolute cowardice, many deeds of treachery and many deeds of honour on both sides. There was Murrough, finally in his element, bellowing like a bull as he sliced his way through the shield wall to get to the King of Leinster. Warriors fell in his path like corn being reaped. There was Brodir, his hair and bearskins flying, looking as if he himself had become a bear, with the strength and savagery of a wild animal. As the battle shook the sands of Clontarf, Dara felt as if the land itself was a great beast, trying to shake off these pesky mortals, like flies from a cow's hide in the green leafy days of summer.

There were times during the battle when Dara did not have any idea who he was fighting – Norseman, Leinsterman, Dubliner – he just kept fighting. Close by, Jarl Sigurd's raven banner was trodden into the sands, falling as its bearer fell. The forces of Brian were slowly bringing the blue banner of Dalcassia closer and closer to the water's edge. Meanwhile, the tide was rising, creeping over the sands, as if coming to meet the Irish. He looked around, hoping to see Niall. There was no sign of him anywhere, and Dara felt his heart sink. But there was Turlough, waving his sword in pursuit of two of the Norse princes, heading towards the weir on the River Tolka. He would go with him and help him. Then they could share the joy of together.

Skari also watched as the raven banner fell, and tried to fight his way nearer the jarl, who was lifting it from the sand, calling on Thorstein to carry it for him.

'It's cursed!' shouted Thorstein. 'I want to get home to my wife and children, I'll not carry it – two have been slain already, bearing it!'

Sigurd drew himself up. 'Very well, then, I will carry my own doom,' he said, and the banner was raised again. But within minutes Murrough had cut his way through the shield wall protecting the jarl. Sigurd went down, Murrough's sword through his heart. The raven banner fell to the sands once more and ravens came to shriek over the Lord of Orkney's body. But Skari had no time to watch, for another Irish soldier was heading his way, screaming curses, his axe drawn and ready to fall on Skari's neck.

And on and on the battle went, and on and on Skari fought, until finally a strange stillness descended. Skari looked around him. There were far more slain men and boys scattered on the battlefield than there were soldiers left fighting. He could see Sigurd's killer, Murrough, lying, desperately wounded nearby, as Anwud of Norway raised his axe in triumph. All around him was clear of the enemy, though he could see his comrades littering the beach as the tide crept up towards their bodies. He saw the amber amulet around Figar's neck. The long scar on Snorri's cheekbone. Some he could not name, there was so much blood everywhere. The smell of blood was vile and the monstrous roaring of the incoming tide filled his head. It was clear that the Irish were winning the battle. Brian's blue banner was moving relentlessly towards the very edge of the shore. He could see a bear-like figure racing for the woods to the west. Was it Brodir, fleeing the battle? Other Norsemen were fleeing, some towards the town, some towards the water. But the tide was rising, and pulling them down into the waves. He had a choice: wait to be slaughtered here by the Irish – or take his chances with the treacherous tide. His father had told him he should try to get home. Yet surely he should stay here and keep fighting, even though the Norse cause was lost?

But now there was a figure racing towards him, wildly waving his sword. It was the Irish boy, the one who looked so much like him. The one who was his brother. He held up his sword but suddenly realised that the boy was not pursuing him, but going to help the young prince Turlough. Turlough was racing after two Norse princes, who were running towards the weir in the Tolka River. But as the four boys reached the water, a great wave came up the river, with a roar like a bull or a clap of thunder. The wave caught the boys just as they tried to cross the weir. Skari stopped in his tracks and blinked. Irish and Norse – all had disappeared. And as Skari watched they did not rise again.

He ran as fast as he could towards the river. Looking down into the water he could see no sign of any of the boys. They could have been carried out with the wave, or their bodies could be crashing against the weir, caught on the land side of the wooden barrier. Skari threw down his shield and his sword, took a deep breath, and dived into the dark pool.

Down, down he went into the water, peering through the greenness. He could just about make out a figure struggling in the water. Moving through the water was painfully slow, for the river was full of water weeds. And now Skari felt his breath running out. His body was pushed against a wooden wall, and he realised he was up against the weir itself. Suddenly the flow brought a face bobbing towards him. It was the young prince, Turlough, his body caught on a holly spike and his blood staining the water as Skari swam towards him, feeling as if his lungs were going to burst. Turlough's fists were knotted tightly into the long hair of the two Norse warriors he had been pursuing. All three were dead. Skari tried to pull Turlough loose from where he was caught; but the wood came away from the weir and Skari could do nothing more as the prince's body floated slowly upwards, his hands still clutching the hair of his enemies.

Skari surfaced, gasping for breath, wondering what impulse had made him dive into the pool. Whatever it was, as soon as he had filled his lungs with air he dived again, once again deep down into the murky greenness. And there, down at the bottom of the pool, was Dara. His lay on the riverbed with his eyes open, doing nothing to save himself – probably unconscious, close to drowning. His brother. His blood. Skari had a choice: by the laws of battle the enemy should be left to die; by the laws of blood he should save one of his family. He did not hesitate: he knew he had to save this Irish savage, this mortal enemy, from death.

He dived down to the bed of the river and caught Dara under the arms. Within moments he had realised that saving the boy might cost him his own life, for Dara was a dead weight, dragging on him, pulling him down into icy blackness. There was a moment when he felt he wanted to be dragged down, to give up everything and breathe in water and night. Should he go down into darkness and cold? Or go up into light and warmth? Something made him give a last convulsive effort, and he kicked his way upwards, his arms still clasped under the shoulders of his Irish half-brother. He dragged himself onto the riverbank and felt the world go black.

CHAPTER 18

THE WITCH IN THE WOOD

Elva pulled her cloak closer around her. This forest to the north of the river was very different from the woods around Kilmainham. Or was it simply that she was noticing things she had not seen before? Noticing how the light came slanting through the branches of the trees and how very green the leaves were. Green fire, she thought, they are like green fire. The brightness of the air made the forest seem almost alive, a shimmering, dancing thing. She glanced down at the ring she wore. It shone gold-red against the greenness, like a tiny flame wrapped around her finger. The air was warm now, and she no longer felt the chill of the water on her wet feet; the droplets on the tall grasses and young ferns glowed like diamonds in the light filtering through the trees. How beautiful this is, she thought. I never want to see the world any other way. This is so wonderful, this must be what Arna feels when she has been pulled into the magical heart of things. No wonder she doesn't want to see the world with ordinary eyes again. No wonder she doesn't want to come down to the place where there is so much ugliness and pain. A swan flew far above the thickets of the wood. Beautiful, savage birds. She remembered her mother's warning: be careful of that other world.

She sat down on a fallen trunk, trying to think. But within moments she noticed something very strange: the tree trunk she was sitting on was starting to smoulder; in a moment it would be aflame. She moved quickly away. And then she noticed that where she had placed her feet there were black marks on the earth. When she looked back she saw that a path of charred grass followed her trail through the forest. And her finger, the one that wore the ring, felt as if it was on fire. She pulled off the ring and immediately the burning stopped. The ring looked smooth and harmless in the palm of her hand. But with this ring I could set the world on fire if I wished, she thought. I could burn the whole city of Dublin, use its straw roofs as a tinderbox and watch the flames grow. I could even, she thought, burn this forest down, turn the trees into burning beacons, if I became angry enough. And this is only a tiny part of Tomar's Ring. No wonder Kormlada wants it. For a woman who loves destruction it is the perfect weapon. If she gets it, surely all Ireland will burn.

Now the brightness had gone and she was cold, but she could not risk putting the ring on again. She made her way carefully through the trees, wishing she had some idea of what she would find at the circle of Tomar. Now she no longer wore the ring, her spirits dropped and she realised that she really had no idea how she would save Arna or defeat Kormlada. And fear came back, that cold creeping feeling of being helpless against the dark power of the queen. But stronger than her fear was the pain in her heart when she thought of losing Arna to the dark air, to the birds of battle, to the other world. She rested again for a moment. And as she sat she heard something, a low buzz, not that of birdsong or bees. It was a human voice, chanting, and it seemed to come from the north of where she was sitting. She made her way as cautiously as she could through the branches, wishing she had not worn her orange cloak – it would stand out like a beacon against the green of the wood. The ground rose here, and she realised that she must be quite close to the edge of the forest, for the light was coming strongly through the trees and there was the smell of the sea in the air. The trees opened out: there was a tent, and an Irish soldier, intent on watching the coastline, which was just visible through the trees. And there was also a very old man with white hair and a gold circlet on his head. He was praying before an altar, and he had his back to her. Her breath caught in her throat. She gasped and the man turned towards her. His face was kind and wise and full of sorrow.

'Who are you, child?' he asked. 'Why do you come here? What do you seek?'

'I'm looking for my sister,' Elva stuttered. The soldier had lurched towards her and stood with his sword raised.

The old man spoke. 'Do not worry, Laidean, and put your sword away. This child means no harm. Child, why do you seek your sister here?'

'The queen, Kormlada, took her away. She means to hurt her, I know it. She has bewitched her. She means to use her to get more power for herself.'

The old king looked even more weary. 'Ah, Kormlada, my dark queen. Always, always, seeking to destroy. Always weaving her webs of darkness. You know that you go into great danger if you seek her, child.'

'I know, but I have to do it, I have to save Arna.'

'Then we can but hope that your sister wishes to be saved. I can give you no more advice than to be careful, and do not listen to anything Kormlada might say. For her oaths are false and her promises mean nothing, as I have learned to my cost. Go on now, child, the place she will be is Tomar's Grove, the ancient magic place – go north through the woods. It is not far. And take my blessing with you. I will pray that you will save your sister.' He placed his hands gently on Elva's head and, closing his eyes, murmured some words. Elva left the grove and made her way northwards.

Within a few minutes she began to feel very cold. The wood began to open out into a dark grove, and at the same time a mist fell. There was the smell of blood, and the trees, hacked and torn, loomed out of the cold fog that enveloped the place. Elva slipped on her ring to stop the chill, but when she did, something very strange happened – she saw, lurking between the desecrated trees, grey, ghostly figures, the spirits of men and women who stayed bound to the grove, trapped by the pain they had suffered there. She tried not to see them, but they watched her, pale and sad. Webs, huge webs, hung down from the branches of the trees, stroking her face and catching at her hair, as if they wanted to catch her, catch her and tie her to themselves like an ancient sacrifice. As if the ghostly people wanted her with them forever.

In the centre of the dark ring of trees, charred and broken, stood a wooden altar, battered and scarred as though hacked with axes. Its base was made of the trunks of huge, ancient oaks. And standing by the altar was Kormlada, dressed in red and black, and before her sat Arna, in her white cloak of feathers, the necklace around her neck. Her sister was smiling, a sweet, meaningless smile. But Kormlada seemed angry about something; she was pacing up and down impatiently. Elva listened hard.

'First, you do not bring me the sword, and now this! Why

is the ring not working? There is something missing, some part of it. I cannot fix it to the altar – there must be another ring to attach it with. What did you do with it? Are you hiding something from me? Did you dare defy me? For if you think to do so, you will suffer for it!'

Arna shook her head. When she spoke her voice was shaking. 'I never had another part, I never saw one.'

'Did anyone else look in the trunk?'

'Maybe Elva did – I never know what she gets up to. I don't know.'

'Elva, that little witch? Why didn't you say that before! We need her here too. You must go back to Dublin and get her to come here, or you will never fly with your Sisters!'

Elva stepped out from the brushwood. 'You don't have to send her back to Dublin. I'm here! But you are not getting the ring from me!'

As she spoke, Elva raised her hand, showing the ring on her middle finger. It spit out sparks of fire when she held it up. 'There now, try and get that! It will burn you if you come near it!'

Kormlada smiled. 'Ah, so it might, but it will not burn Arna. And you, Arna, you now have a last chance to prove yourself. You were weak when I sent you to kill the boy and take the broken sword, but now you must be strong. The ring and the sword need blood to make them work to my purpose. You did not kill the boy: instead you must kill your sister, and then you will be truly worthy to become one of the Valkyries!'

She went to Arna and pulled her upright. Then she wrapped the girl's fingers around the dagger she drew from her belt. 'Go, you know you hate her. Kill her!'

Arna looked at Elva and raised her hands. She began to walk towards her, her face still blank, her eyes dead, the dagger held upright in both her hands. Elva knew she should move, and move fast, but her feet felt glued to the ground. She gasped out, her voice a whisper:

'No, Arna, no, you can't hurt me! I'm your sister, remember!'

Arna paused. Her expression became puzzled, as if trying to remember something from very long ago. 'My sister? But my Sisters are the battle maidens.'

'Maybe they are. But you have another sister. Me! Try to remember, Arna – remember Weland and the forge and Birgit and all of us. Remember Astrid giving out and Rolf and the stories by the fireside. Come back to us!'

'Ah, I remember ... something ... But it's sad, it's all gone ... it's too late ...' There were tears in Arna's eyes.

Kormlada cut in furiously: 'No tears, no tears! We are not made for tears. Tears are for humans, only humans! Tears are for the world you are going to leave behind. Tears are for the foolish boys who laughed at you, for your foolish sister who does not realise that the one sharing her bread is half Aesir. And if she can kill her human half, she will be fully so, and become one of the Bright Ones. The ones who glory in battle and do not cry for the slain. One of Odin's handmaidens! See how they shine: see how the feathers grow; soon you will have wings and fly with them to the Kingdom of the Air, where nothing can wound you. Arna, stretch out your arms and step forward into *your* kingdom!'

Now the wood was dark and full of rushing wind, of black wings and the saddest of cries: the air around them was as cold as ice.

Don't let me be frozen in the cold, thought Elva: don't let my heart be blown out by this dark wind.

Arna's eyes were no longer silver, but dark red. She moved forward.

'Don't,' whispered Elva, 'Arna, don't hurt me! I can't give you the ring: I can't let that witch have it. It has too much power. Arna, Arna, don't you know me? It's Elva! It's your sister!'

And then, as if struck by a blow to the heart, Arna stopped and looked, and her hands holding the dagger dropped to her sides. The dagger fell among the weeds and the brambles.

'My lady! I can't do it! I wish I could, but I can't,' she said. She fell to the ground, her hands covering her face. Elva rushed towards her but Kormlada was there first, pushing her away.

'Get off her, child of a dog. You have ruined my plans,' she screamed.

She took up some whitethorn rods that lay in a bundle on the altar and rapidly made a circle around Arna, and Elva found she could not move over the invisible line. With a cry, Arna fell forward so that she lay on the ground, unconscious, her face pale as death, her eyes closed.

'See what you have done! You have broken her, killed her with the choice you have made her make. She is half Aesir and can never find a home in the world of your tiny human hearts.'

'But she can't be dead! There must be a way to save her!'

Kormlada's eyes grew cunning. 'You would do anything for her, would you not? So maybe all is not lost. I can help her, you know. Perhaps I can wake her from her sleep. But I need you to do something for me. First, give me the ring.'

Elva shook her head wordlessly.

'Give me the ring, I said.'

'I will give you the ring when Arna wakes up, not before.'

Kormlada let out a hiss of rage.

'You are as stubborn as a block of wood, you dogchild. Very well, if you will not do that, you will do something else for me. You must go to the sands of Clontarf and look among the bodies for the Orkney prince, Skari, and the Irish prince, Dara. Skari now has the blade of a broken sword; Dara holds the hilt of that same sword. You must bring them both here, for it is the sword of Carlus. It and the Ring of Tomar were stolen from this place when the Irish burnt and hacked the grove. They give great power to whoever holds them ... I will take them and rule the land!'

'But King Brian is the high king, and he is still alive!'

There was a sneer in Kormlada's voice when she replied. 'Don't you worry your little head about that. Brian is an old man and I am sure I can arrange something for him. Get you gone now: the longer Arna remains in that death-sleep the harder it will be to wake her!'

As Elva ran through the thickets towards the shore, she could hear her sister's voice in her head:

I'm sorry I got us into this mess, she promised me that I would be able to go with the Valkyries if I did what she wanted. She showed them to me in the smoke of her fire.

I know, Arna, I know. I think I understand. But it was only her trickster magic, not your real Sisters that you saw. She just wanted you to do her bidding ...

I know that now. She told me I could be like that forever, if I did what she wanted, find the broken sword in the Irish camp and bring it to her. But I could not kill the boy. And I could not kill you. And now she wants my blood, to feed the spirits and make an army of ghosts, of after-walkers ...

But she won't get it. I promise you. Arna, I am going to save you. Somehow.

CHAPTER 19

AT THE WEIR OF THE TOLKA

Dara woke lying on the ground. He sat up. The sun was beginning to set behind Tomar's Wood; the trees looked as if they were on fire. Around him was desolation: bodies upon bodies, death upon death, ravens swooping down to perch on dead men's skulls. The air smelt of blood and salt. The waters of the river and sea were red with blood and the scattered remains of so many dead. The sea lapped at the shoreline, carrying the bodies back and forth in the tide. In the distance, a few lonely figures of Norsemen disappeared into the sea. They would have little chance of reaching the ships that now bobbed far out on the tide, thought Dara. Some men held dead companions in their arms, some rolled on the ground, hoping against hope that the movement might ease their pain. Beside him was the Orkney boy, his face as pale as death.

As he watched, Skari opened his eyes. One green, one blue.

There was silence for a moment, and then Dara spoke. 'I remember. The water … you saved me,' he said. 'You saved my life.'

Skari nodded. 'You didn't kill me, in the wood, when you could have. You saved my life too,' he said. 'And you are … you are …'

Dara nodded, wincing as he moved his head. 'I am your half-brother. You mother is my mother.'

'How do you know about me?'

Dara shook his head, trying to clear the fuzziness in his brain. 'I worked it out after Cormac acted so strangely when we met in the wood. And my mother – our mother – has been waking at night for years, crying out for her lost child.'

'What's she like, our mother?'

Dara shrugged. 'Like any mother, I suppose. She fusses a lot. But she's not the worst. She has the same eyes as us.'

The two boys looked at each other for a long moment, both suddenly shy of each other. Then Dara staggered onto his knees and crawled to where three figures lay, crumpled on the sand, their bodies carried in by the tide.

'It's Turlough,' he said. He gently untangled Turlough's hands from where he still held on to the hair of the two Norse boys. Then he turned the body over. There was a wooden stake through his friend's heart. He sank to his knees and tried to pull it out, but he fell back, panting with the effort.

Skari said: 'He was caught in the weir of Clontarf. I tried to pull him free but he was already dead. I think he died because he would not let go of the two Norse soldiers – they dragged him down. The stake is from the weir, it came loose in the struggle. I'm sorry. He was a brave prince. He was a good friend of yours?'

'He was like a brother to me,' said Dara.

But now they noticed a small figure, dressed in a saffron cloak, running towards them from the wood.

'It's the Dublin girl,' said Skari.

Elva had been crying with pain and panic, but when she saw the two boys, her face broke into a wide smile.

'You are alive! Both of you! Oh this is wonderful! But you have to help me. You must help me save Arna!'

'Who's Arna?' asked Dara.

'My sister. Queen Kormlada has her, and she has sent me to get you and the blade and hilt of the sword you carry. She means to do terrible things with it and the ring! We have to make a plan: we have to be really clever about this. I'm sure she will kill Arna if she gets the sword and the ring together, and use her blood to raise the spirits of the wood. Come with me quickly, I'll tell you everything as we go!'

Dara tried to stand, but his feet collapsed underneath him.

'I… I'm not sure I am able to walk,' he said, furious with himself. His face felt like ice; it was blue from the freezing water. But Elva turned the ring on her finger, and then she passed her hands over Dara's face. At once, Dara's face was warmed by a flame which did not burn.

'Now,' said Elva impatiently. 'Now, you must both come with me.'

'You don't expect me to help the Irish, do you?' said Skari.

'I'm not doing this to help the Irish,' said Elva, 'I'm doing it to stop Kormlada taking over everything! She and Brodir will rule Ireland! And we have to save Arna.'

Skari thought of Arna's pale, sad face. He thought of Brodir's savagery and Kormlada's lies. 'Brodir of Man?' he said in disgust. 'If he and Kormlada are in this together, I'll help you whatever way I can.'

Dara broke in: 'But I cannot leave the battle. I must continue to fight – I owe it to my people and to Turlough. I can't leave. It's the warrior's code.'

Elva snorted with frustration. 'Look around you – the battle is over. King Brian's troops have won. Why do you think it is more noble to stay here and kill more people than to save a life? I'm telling you, the real battle is in the forest now, against the queen! Arna must be saved or all of us will be governed by Kormlada and Brodir!'

Dara said nothing. He just stared around him in horror at the destruction everywhere.

CHAPTER 20

THE RING OF TOMAR

Standing at the altar in Tomar's Grove, looking at Kormlada's cruel face, Skari wondered how he could ever have thought her beautiful. At her feet was Arna, lying quietly on the ground, a circle of bare thorn branches surrounding her. Kormlada had bound her hair with herbs, and white and black feathers lay across her mouth and nose, marking her face with strange symbols. Her eyes were closed, and he could not see if she was still breathing. Kormlada laughed gleefully when she saw them approaching.

'So my ducklings have come home to roost! This is a delight! But where is the Irish boy?'

Elva said shakily: 'He's dead. But we have his part of the sword.'

'You are lying,' said Kormlada. 'He is alive, somewhere. But no matter, the sword is the important thing. First, girl, give me the ring.'

Elva shook her head. She hid her hands in her cloak. 'King Brian told me never to believe anything you say. I want to see Arna awake and free first.'

Kormlada hissed with anger. 'She will never get free if you do not give me the ring! Come, give it me!' She advanced towards Elva. Skari too moved forward. Just as Kormlada reached Elva, Elva drew her arm out from under her cloak: in it was the sword, hilt and blade fitted together and welded by the magic of the fire ring. Elva struck the queen as hard as she could, and Kormlada fell back, her shoulder wounded. Quick as lightning, Skari had her hands bound and Dara, who had crept up behind her, tied a strip from Elva's cloak tightly around her mouth. Then Skari dived for the queen's feet, and held them tight while Dara tied them together. The two boys prevented her from any further movement by sitting on her. Meanwhile, Elva had unclasped the ring from Arna's neck, and, with shaking fingers, attached her small ring to the clasp. And while Kormlada thrashed her head and body furiously, the Ring of Tomar was closed around her neck and, using all their strength, the children lifted the queen upwards. The small ring was pushed over the iron stake that was set upright in the altar. The queen could not move her neck; her feet could not touch the ground. She was left caught and wriggling like a fish on a line.

'Well, that's put a stop to your spells and lying words!' said Elva with satisfaction. But then she looked over at Arna. 'My sister looks so pale. Arna, can you hear us?'

There was no answer from her sister.

And then Dara, with a knowledge coming from he knew not where, went to where Arna lay, still unmoving, and he pulled the ring of whitethorn from around her. Then he gently unbound the foul herbs that Kormlada had woven into her hair and pulled away the feathers from where they blocked her mouth and her nose and her ears. Then Skari filled his hands with water from the stream, and he washed Arna's face free of the marks that Kormlada had made on it with blood and earth. Elva rubbed her sister's cheeks with her hands and the terrible whiteness left Arna's face, and there was life in her eyes again. She pulled herself up, and the cloak of feathers fell away from her.

'What happened?' she asked. 'I can't remember anything – just that Kormlada was going to do some terrible harm ...'

'She was going to kill you,' said Dara bluntly. 'She wanted your blood to raise the spirits of the ring and the sword, so that she could send them to battle and rule all of us, with Brodir.'

'And you saved me ...' Arna was looking intently at Elva.

Elva said: 'Well, between us we did … I had the sword and Dara crept up behind her … though he took some convincing … he's stubborn, so he is … it was only when I asked him did he not know what it was like to lose a brother or sister that he agreed to help.'

'And he insisted on being the one to do the creeping up behind. I should have been the one to do that, as the eldest,' Skari interrupted.

'But you would have made as much noise as a herd of horses!' Dara cut in.

Elva laughed. 'Don't they sound like brothers already!'

The two boys looked at each other and laughed too. And there was, for the first time in many months, a shaky laugh from Arna, although she was not sure what she was laughing about. She pulled herself over to where Elva knelt beside her and hugged her tightly. Her eyes filled with tears.

'I've been so stupid, Elva,' she said. 'I'm sorry.'

As the two sisters hugged each other, and the two boys looked away, embarrassed, the wood was suddenly filled with an unearthly howl. The children looked over at Kormlada, but her mouth was still gagged and the knots they had made bound her tight. There was the sound again … it shook the wood and the children stared at each other, their skin prickling in fear. It was the sound of pure sorrow. For each of them it brought back the worst of times – for Dara it was his mother crying in the night, for Arna it was her own heart breaking for the mother she had never really known.

Then Dara shook himself. 'We must find the high king, we must find King Brian. Something terrible has happened to him! That's the voice of the banshee!'

The children looked at each other in consternation.

'I know where he is!' cried Elva. 'Follow me.'

They ran from the grove, the queen's eyes flashing curses at them from the altar. The thickets were now dark and cold, for the sun had set. When they arrived at the grove where Brian had been praying, they stopped abruptly. The king was there, but he was no longer kneeling at prayer. He was lying on a bier of green branches, a peaceful look on his face, a crucifix clasped in his hands. Around him stood his kinsmen and a handful of the captains of the Irish army. Cormac was there and he gave a faint, sad smile when he saw Dara.

'There he lies, as if asleep, our lost king, our very greatest king. He was truly the gate of battle and the sheltering tree to us all. Where shall we shelter now?'

King Malachy of Meath was also there. There was a strange expression on his face as he looked at the body of the high king.

Tadhg, one of Brian's sons, looked at him suspiciously. 'Why didn't you come sooner to help us in the battle? Why did you only come in at the end, when Murrough had been killed and the Norse were already retreating?'

'I would have come earlier,' Malachy's voice was hoarse,

'but my men were trapped. We were surrounded by a strange red fog. I swear to you, if my own brother had been standing beside me, I would not have recognised him. We could not move, and as we stood we were battered by the bitterest wind I have ever encountered. I cannot explain it. It felt as if it was carrying the very blood of the battle into our eyes to blind us, and the long locks of hair of those who died were wrapping themselves around us, binding us to the earth. And it tied us to each other, so none of us could move. And then suddenly it all stopped; we could see and we were free of the entanglement. It must have been some witchery of the Norse.'

The children looked at each other with wide eyes. Could the red mist have been Kormlada's doing?

But Tadhg did not look convinced. 'So the watcher from the distance gains much and risks little!' he muttered, turning his back on Malachy and walking away into the forest.

Now they saw that Ospak had also survived the battle, but his face was pale and his eyes full of pain. He stood by another body. Brodir's corpse had been left upright, propped against a tree and surrounded by the ring of thorny branches the Irish had used to capture him. His long black hair was streaming over the wounds on his body; his eyes were open and wild. His body seemed half-covered in fur. His sword was in his right hand, but at the end of his left arm there was no hand, but a single deadly claw. The guard that had been too late to save Brian from Brodir's sword had made sure that the killer of the king would not escape. Skari remembered the bear-like figure he had seen leaving the battlefield. It seemed that Brodir had made for the refuge of the wood, and found the king alone except for Laidean. He had killed him with a single blow, as Brian knelt at prayer.

The children turned away in horror from the sight. Then Elva spotted a familiar figure coming towards them through the trees.

She ran to him. 'You're better! You're not sick anymore!'

Weland shook his head. 'Indeed I am. I fear it was magic had me tied to my bed. And whatever it was, it is defeated now!' He hugged Elva tightly. But now Arna had also flung herself into his arms and was hugged and kissed in her turn.

'I thought I had lost you, my little daughters,' said Weland. 'I thought I had lost you both.'

Then there was a shriek of joy as Birgit appeared through the trees. The girls were hugged and kissed and cried over once again. When she heard the story of how Dara and Skari had helped to save her children, they got the same treatment from her, while Weland clapped them on their shoulders and congratulated them on their courage.

'Father,' said Arna, 'the queen – we left her in Tomar's Grove. She–'

Weland put his finger to his lips.

'Say nothing here, let's go and see what's happening. She'll be killed if the Irish get hold of her, and although she is a troll-wife, I don't want her blood on my hands. Enough blood has been spilt today.'

They went quickly to the grove. But there was no sign of the queen. The stake still held the ring, and the sword still lay on the altar where Elva had thrown it.

Weland looked intently at the stake and shook his head. 'Who knows what happened? Perhaps the Morrigan took her, she has called on her often enough. Or perhaps Odin has taken her away to be with the spirits she tried to rise against his will. But whatever happened, I can only hope that we'll see no more of her in Dublin.'

Arna said: 'Look, Father, the rings are still here; and the sword. We left them when we heard the banshee.'

'Aye, and here they should remain, though the trees are cut and the shrine is broken. We'll bury the sword deep in the earth and sink the rings in the water of the well. Let them remain there so no harm can be done with them. No, Dara, do not look like that. I know you would like to keep the sword, but its powers are too great for you to control. Perhaps when you're all older you will come back to find what is buried and drowned.'

So they took the ring and the sword, and the ring was sunk in the dark pool by the altar, and the sword buried deep in the earth beside it. And when they had done that, Arna said, with wonder in her voice, 'Look, everyone, look at the wood of the altar!'

There, at the base of the oak trunks of the altar, hacked and beaten as they were, tiny shoots were starting to grow, bright green and gold as the sun.

Weland said: 'So, our work here is done. Let's leave this place to heal itself. Now, Dara, you should get back to your companions and your family. There are many wounded that need our help.'

Dara nodded, and looked at Skari. 'Skari, you are half Dalcassian. Do you want to come back with me? Back to Dalcassia? To meet your clan, to see your mother? She'll be so happy to meet you!'

Skari tried to think. It was hard, because his heart was in such turmoil. Too much had happened today. He had found his brother and discovered that his mother was still alive. And he had lost his father, a loss that he still hadn't really been able to take in. But now the thought of the long journey home, and life without Ragnall, seemed very hard. Maybe it would be easier not to go back. He could make a new life with these brave Dalcassians, with his brother and his mother. Imagine meeting his real mother at last! He had so many questions to ask her. He had thought she was lost to him forever. But to do that would be to leave his people and his place. He thought of his father's last wish: he had asked him to go back and be lord in his place. He thought of Ingrid, watching, waiting to see the ships sail into the harbour at Birsay, waiting for his father come back. She would be very lonely without Ragnall. And she had looked after Skari from the time he was tiny. She had taught him to walk and talk. If anyone was his mother, it was Ingrid. And he had a promise to keep to little Gudrun. He shook his head.

Weland said: 'Well, we must go back into the city. Skari, you can come with us. As long as you are with me you're safe.'

'How is it you walk safely in the Irish camp?' asked Skari.

'The Irish have some respect for me, and for Birgit's healing powers. They need a smith to reforge their broken weapons, and a healer for their broken bodies, so our house is always held in honour. And so I can stand over your safety, Skari, for as long as you wish to stay with me. You're welcome to make your home in Dublin, if that is what you wish. But I see you do not.'

Skari shook his head. 'I promised my father I would return to our land and to my mother. And to our people. I must lead them now. But how will I get back to the ships – if there are any at all left with a crew still alive?'

Weland smiled. 'There I can help you. I will row you out, for the handful of ships that remain will not leave until the tide goes out tonight. That is, if you're sure you want to go.'

Skari nodded. 'I'll be sad to leave you all, but I must go.'

Arna suddenly grasped her father's arm. 'Father, let me go too. Let me go with the Norsemen – not to Orkney, but to the far north, where perhaps I can find my mother and my people.'

Weland looked at his daughter with anxious eyes. 'Are you still dreaming of becoming a Valkyrie, of riding to battle with Odin? You have too much human blood in you for that, you know that now, don't you? You know that the queen deceived you with dreams of flying with the swan maidens?'

Arna nodded. 'I do know that. But I also know that my mother was Aesir, and your blood has that in it which is not fully human either. I will never be happy living an ordinary life here in Dublin. Let me go, father, let me take my mother's cloak for protection and go to find my fate.'

Birgit said: 'But Arna, we don't want to lose you. And you're still so young! How will you make your way in the world all alone?'

'I … I have learned much. I have learned that my fate is a strange one, and I must go to meet it. I can never be content until I start the journey.'

Weland's voice was very weary. 'It is true you have the blood of the Aesir, the elves, in your veins. And it is true it is hard to know how you could ever be happy in our town. Your mother was the same. I thought to hold her, but her blood called her to the cold and wild places of the north. Arna, you are indeed one whose fate will not be a common one.'

Elva grasped her sister's arm: 'But I don't want you to go! I feel like I have only just found you, and now you want to go away again!'

Arna laughed and hugged Elva: 'Oh, little sister, don't

worry. I'll come back and visit you, one way or another. You too have powers that are not ordinary – you have been brave and steadfast and I'm sure your fate will not be a common one either! Please Father, Mother, tell me I may go!'

Weland and Birgit looked at each other. Then Birgit nodded, very slowly, and Weland let out a great sigh. 'Very well, then. We'll make plans for tonight. Dara, we must bring you back to your people. Your father will be worrying.'

Dara drew a deep breath. He had been afraid to even think about his father. 'He is alive?' His voice came out more of a squeak than he would have liked.

'Yes. He's wounded, but not badly. Your father will be one of those that will bear Brian to Armagh, where the king wished to be buried.'

As they walked through the wood, Elva tried her best not to cry. It didn't work too well. She took Arna's sleeve and whispered to her: 'I thought you would come home with me and we could be real sisters at last.'

'Elva, we are sisters. Real sisters. I'll think of you often and perhaps, when I've found what I'm looking for, I'll come back. One day you'll hear a knock on the door in Dublin and when you open it, it will be me standing there.'

'Or it might be me!' said Skari. 'Maybe I'll go on my travels and come to Dublin too!' He was smiling as he spoke.

'Or even me,' broke in Dara. 'If they let the Irish in through the gates of Dublin ever again.'

Elva wiped her face and grinned. 'Perhaps I won't be here! Perhaps I will be having some adventures myself, and not be at home waiting by the fire at all. For one thing, I'd like to find out how the boys' mother and Svanhild got hold of the rings and the sword ...'

Skari smiled back at her. 'Perhaps you will. After all, you've already shown that you're a hero. You're bound to have more adventures!'

CHAPTER 21

EASTER SATURDAY–SUNDAY 1014

Although Brian's army had won the battle, it had suffered huge losses. No-one was left with the will to attack the town of Dublin itself, which remained safe and silent behind its walls. While Prince Donagh, still on his way from the mountains, was now the leader of the army, there was confusion as to who was to be the heir to Brian's kingdom, now that Murrough was dead. The battle that Brian had hoped would end all battles seemed instead to have sown new troubles. But at least the Irish tribes could be sure that the power of the Vikings was broken in Ireland. Now began the weary work of tending to the wounded and burying the slain. Murrough and Turlough were carried from the sands of Clontarf and buried in the ancient graveyard at Kilmainham. A stone was raised over them, and Brodir's sword buried with them, so that none should use it again. It took long hours for the rest of the dead to be buried. Indeed, there were so many that some warriors' bodies were burned on the sands of Clontarf, their funeral pyres lighting the dark sky above.

Dara did not rest. As long as he kept working he could keep his sorrow for King Brian and Turlough at bay. Every time he thought of never seeing either of them again he felt choked with grief. But it helped a little when he found that Niall had survived the battle, though he was wounded. He was still well able to talk, though, and regaled Dara with stories of the Leinster soldiers he had fought. 'I'll tell old Diarmuid when we get back to Killaloe that I didn't do too badly for someone with two left arms and two left feet!'

Dara's father was up and about already, planning the journey to take King Brian to Armagh, where he was to be buried in the cathedral. When he saw how pale Dara was, he came over to him and told him to stop working or he would collapse from tiredness.

'Come with me to the king's bier,' he said. 'We must pray for him.' So they stood silently by the bier, looking at the king's pale and peaceful face. Dara finally felt the tears roll down his cheeks. His father put his arm around his shoulder.

'If I were a great king, and too old to go into battle, I think that is the way I would wish to die, with news of the victory coming in as I prayed for my people. I know it is sad, but it is not the worst of deaths. His name will be remembered, always, with great honour, for we are safe now from being part of a Viking empire, ruled from beyond the seas by those whose ways are not ours. And thanks to you and your friends, we're safe from something worse – being ruled by black magic, by a witch and a thug!'

That evening, Arna and Skari, with Elva accompanying them, were ferried out into the bay by Weland, and put on board the solitary ship left to travel back to the Orkneys. From there, Arna planned to find passage to the far north. Skari was welcomed with open arms; he was now a lord of his people, and he felt the weight of that responsibility as he boarded the boat. But then the sail was set and the boat began its journey northwards. Feeling the motion of the boat under his feet, Skari realised how good it was to be at sea again. And how very good it was to be heading home. He thought of Ingrid, stalwart against the bitter wind, climbing the heights of Lambsfell to rescue motherless lambs. And Gudrun, using a cow's horn as a bottle, nursing those lambs to health by the fire in the great hall. The salt wind came from the southwest, pushing them north and east. The moon was waning, hidden sometimes by the patches of sea mist which drifted across the sky. Skari took a deep breath. He was a Viking. This was his element.

Arna stood beside him in the stern, also breathing in the wind and the smell of the sea. Dublin was behind them, and the roar of the tide sent its last message of farewell to the two of them. Skari wondered if he would see his half-brother again, or Elva, and looked back, though only once. But Arna's face was turned towards the night sky and the wheeling gulls, as if they were sending her a message that only she could understand.

As they watched the boat carry Arna and Skari away from them into the mist, Elva's face was wet with tears. Weland sighed and took up the oars, turning the boat towards land. 'Well, child, you are the only daughter with us now. We must get back to Dublin.'

Elva nodded. She couldn't speak.

Arna was gone, and Elva might never see her again. But in some way her sister was closer to her now than she had ever been. And although she no longer wore the fire ring it seemed that she could still see beyond, into the spirit world. For as she watched the boat sailing into the silver path of moonlight, it seemed to her that it was not alone. A ghostly company of noble ships sailed with it on its voyage home.

Their own little boat made its way quietly towards the city. There were no lights showing in Dublin this evening, but the city was calm, as if a great storm had passed. As they reached the shoreline, where the light of the funeral pyres was fading, Elva thought she could see a figure on a grey horse galloping northwards along the sands of Clontarf. Sparks of fire flew from the horse's hooves. But then the image was lost in the sea mist and it was too late to be sure of what she had seen.

Later, deep into the night, Dara woke. The Easter bonfire, usually a scene of great joy, had been lit in silence. The bell of the ruined church had been rung, not in celebration but in mourning for the dead. The priests had sung the prayers for the lost ones, their chanting echoed by the soft cooing of the doves gathered in the trees above the old grey walls. Dara lay against his father's shoulder, both of them wrapped in his tattered green cloak, propped against an oak tree. His father's last words to him before he had fallen asleep echoed in his mind: 'Ah, Dara, how could I have faced your mother if I had lost you to the water? How could I have lived with myself? Whatever grace has kept you safe, rescued you from drowning, we must always give thanks for it.'

Dara had said nothing, just hugged his father tighter. But he thought how strange it was that it had been the brother he had never known, the enemy soldier, who had saved his life.

Before them lay the earthen mounds that had been raised over the dead men and boys, and covered with forest flowers and green ferns. For a while Dara kept watch, as if guarding the soldiers that lay sleeping and at peace in the shadow of the monastery walls. Their swords marked the green mounds where they lay, piercing the soil. Hilt upright they stood, so that they formed crosses, shining in the moonlight. Dara snuggled closer into the shelter of his father's cloak, and fell back into sleep. Tomorrow would begin the long march to Armagh, and the longer march south. But at the end of the march would be home.

HISTORICAL NOTE

The Battle of Clontarf is a historical event so enmeshed in folklore that it is hard to know where the story ends and the history begins. We do know that the battle took place on 23 April 1014. We know that it was fought on the sands of Clontarf and the surrounding areas of Marino, Fairview and Phibsboro. Over ten thousand soldiers fought in the battle and the casualties were enormous. The opposing sides were the forces of Brian Boru, high king of Ireland, leading an army of mainly Munster and Connacht soldiers, and the Leinster and Viking forces, led by Mael Mordha of Leinster. The Leinster forces were aided by Norse soldiers from beyond the seas, including the troops of Jarl Sigurd of Orkney and Brodir of Man. The Norse of Dublin under King Sitric Silkbeard, also supported Mael Mordha. King Malachy of Meath had come south to fight with King Brian, but did not join in the battle until very late in the day.

The immediate cause of the battle was a disagreement

between Brian and Mael Mordha, perhaps incited by King Brian's ex-wife, Gormflaith – or Kormlada, as she was known to the Norse. However, it was one of a number of battles in which the various kings of Ireland fought with each other for the high kingship and, occasionally, with the Norse for control of their five city kingdoms. Despite the fact that the Leinster-Norse forces were stronger in numbers, Brian's army was victorious, although he himself was killed. The Battle of Clontarf ended any possibility of Ireland becoming a Norse colony, dominated by that culture or ruled by its laws.

After this point, the storytellers on both sides take over, telling strange tales of magic banners, weaving women, banshees, boiling bloodstorms and demonic ravens. *Blood Brother, Swan Sister*, while based on the facts of the battle – as far as we know them – is part of this tradition, using the folklore surrounding the event to create a new version of the tale. I have also woven in other Norse folklore and myth where it seemed to fit with the story. Tomar's Grove existed, and was burned by Malachy of Meath. The sword of Carlus and the Ring of Tomar, both sacred to the Norse of Dublin, were taken by Malachy. Queen Gormflaith, or Kormlada, the ex-wife of Brian and of Malachy of Meath, the mother of Sitric of Dublin and the sister of Mael Mordha does indeed seem to have been a powerful player in the lead-up to the battle, but there is no evidence that she wanted to take control of the kingdom of Ireland, either by political or magical means.

She had, however, promised to marry both Sigurd of Orkney and Brodir of Man if Brian's forces were defeated.

Of the other main characters in the story, almost all existed apart from Dara, Arna, Elva, Skari and their families. Turlough did indeed die with his hands still caught in the hair of two Viking princes; Brodir killed Brian and was in turn killed by the Irish; and Sigurd died holding the banner that had been woven to protect him but carried a curse.

If you are interested in knowing more about the battle, accounts can be found in the modern translations of the chronicles of the time. On the Irish side, the main account is *The War of the Gael and the Foreigners* and the main Norse account is in *The Saga of Burnt Njal*, from which the Valkyries' song in *Blood Brother, Swan Sister* is taken.

OTHER BOOKS BY EITHNE MASSEY

The Silver Stag of Bunratty

In an Ireland full of conflict and war, four children are determined to prevent Richard de Clare, Lord of Bunratty, from killing the magical Silver Stag and display the head on the walls of the castle. But conflict and danger await the children – as well as extraordinary adventure.

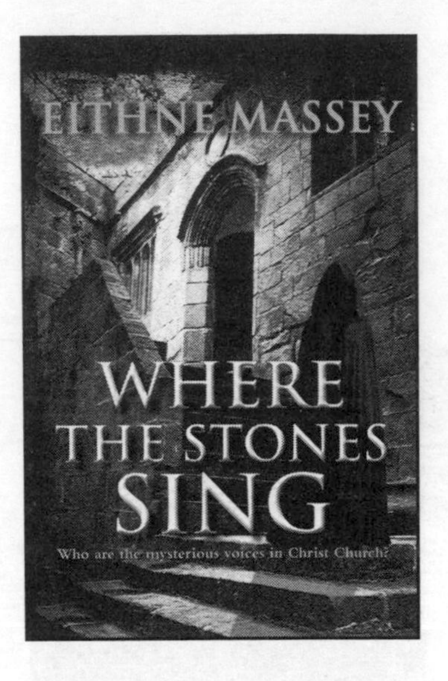

Where the Stones Sing

As the spectre of the Black Death hovers over medieval Dublin, Kai is plucked from the filthy streets to sing in the great Christ Church choir. But Kai has a secret that must be kept hidden, even from new friends. Kai will need great strength, talent and unexpected help just to survive.

The Secret of Kells

When Aidan and his cat Pangur Bán arrive in Kells, Brendan's life becomes very exciting. A deadly wolf-pack, marauding Vikings and the serpent god Crom Cruach all have to be faced and outwitted. And there is also the challenge of the Book of Kells – can it be completed and kept safe from the Vikings?

The Dreaming Tree

Back home in Brazil, Roberto loved playing football. Now he lives in Ireland, and he'd really like to have a game with the boys in the park, but he's too shy. When his granny tells him the Brazilian story of the dreaming tree, he doesn't see how it can help … But maybe it can!

Best-loved Irish Legends

Beautifully told versions of all the favourite legends, with splendid colour illustrations. Includes: The Salmon of Knowledge, How Cú Chulainn Got His Name, The Children of Lir, The King with the Donkey's Ears, Fionn and the Giant. Available in two editions: large size and mini. (Mini edition also available in French and German.)

www.obrien.ie